TUCKAWAY RETREAT TWO

by Karen A. Boxell

Inks and Bindings
888-290-5218
www.inksandbindings.com
orders@inksandbindings.com

CONTENTS

CHAPTER ONE

Thump! Thump! Thump! sounded loudly on the bedroom floor. Carl squirmed down under the covers. He pulled the blanket over his head, gave a deep sigh, and settled into sleep again. Thump! Thump! Thump! sounded again, and more insistent this time. Carl, a lanky fifteen-year-old teenager, pulled the blanket off his head, eyes at half-mast. He turned his head just enough to see his alarm clock on the corner of the bureau. Yep! The clock said it was time to get up. He wished his Mom would get out of the habit of beating up the kitchen ceiling to get his attention. His alarm clock could do the 'getting-up' job just fine, and it was soooo much quieter. He rolled over and pushed the covers aside. His feet hit the cold floor, and he gave a little shiver. It was only March, and winter seemed in no hurry to disappear.

"Brrr!" he whispered to himself. He stood up and reached for the ceiling. One long stretch and he could almost reach it. He wriggled his fingertips. "Got to get the blood flowing," he thought to himself. He took one big step which took him to his bedroom door. He peeked out to see if the bathroom door was open or closed. "Great! It's open," and he slipped down the hall and through the open door just as his 'big' sister, Veronica, came out of her bedroom, headed in the same direction.

"I beat you to it this time," he chortled as he quickly slammed the door. The lock clicked into place.

"You're a beast, you know that?" his sister shouted through the door, and gave it a few smacks. "It's my turn to be first."

"Not if you don't get up in time, it's not," he replied. "I'll save you a little hot water if you just go away and don't bother me. No standing out there banging on the door."

"Okay, this time, but you better be quick," she responded as she gave the door one final smack and headed down the stairs to the kitchen.

"Mornin', Mom," she greeted the young-looking woman in the kitchen. "What's for breakfast?"

"Good morning, sweetheart! I've made some blueberry muffins, and there are plenty of eggs," her mother, Virginia (Ginny), smiled and gave her a brief hug. "What's your choice?"

"I think some scrambled eggs and a muffin will do just fine," she said. "Carl's hogging the shower right now and should be down very soon. He promised not to use all the hot water. We'll see what happens there," she added. "I can always hope."

"Now, he's not that bad. You just have to be a little faster in the morning," her mother sympathized.

"I know! I keep telling myself that, but I just don't do it. My bed feels so comfy, especially on these colder mornings." Veronica plopped down at the table.

"Here you go!" and a plate of eggs with a muffin alongside was set in front of her.

"I'm hungry as a bear waking from its winter nap," Carl's loud voice echoed down the stairs ahead of him and into the kitchen. "What's for breakfast this morning? The bathroom's all yours, Sis! Good morning, Mom!" His blond head and lanky frame appeared in the kitchen behind his string of words. He gave his Mom a quick hug before pulling out a chair and seating himself.

"You took long enough, baby bro'," Veronica said. "Do I have any hot water?"

"Sure! I promised, didn't I?" Carl answered, as his breakfast was set before him, and he scooped up a big forkful of scrambled eggs.

"We'll see how much is left," she replied, as she finished the last of her muffin. She got up from the table, put her empty breakfast dishes in the sink, and left the room.

"Anything happening after school today?" his mother asked him.

"Yeah, soccer tryouts. I think I'll stay for that. Is that okay with you, Mom? I can get a ride home from one of the other kids, so you won't have to leave work to pick me up." Carl looked worriedly at his mother. She had a demanding job managing a gift shop, and afternoons were some of the busiest times. The kids' Dad had died in a military accident a few years ago, and Ginny was the main and only breadwinner right now.

"Yes, of course, that's fine with me. I didn't know you were interested in soccer," she responded with a smile.

Just at that moment. Pinto, the family's black and white cat, jumped up onto Carl's lap. Carl gave his sleek, black fur a long stroke and gently set Pinto on his feet. "You have your own food," he reminded the cat, and scooped another forkful of egg into his own mouth. "Well," he began to explain. "I'm not sure if I am or not, but the soccer coach wants to try out some of us freshmen and see if he can start a junior league. Me and a couple of my friends thought we'd give it a try."

"Certainly, can't hurt to try out," Ginny nodded. "What time do you think you'll be home?"

"It shouldn't be too late. By five o'clock I'm pretty sure," he added.

"Okay! Maybe you can help Ronnie with dinner. There is a meeting scheduled after closing tonight, and I will be late myself," his mom replied. (Ronnie was the family pet name for Veronica, and had become her nickname with her friends as well.)

"Sure, no problem," Carl responded. "We'll think something up." He grabbed his lunch bag off the counter and headed out the door. "Gotta go! See ya tonight!"

Veronica entered the kitchen with her school books stacked in her arms. "Carl's sure in a hurry this morning," she commented.

"Yes, I think he's meeting some friends. He said they were planning to try out for soccer after school today. I have an after-hours meeting tonight. He said he would help you with dinner tonight. Okay?" she queried.

"Yep! We can manage that," Veronica agreed. "I'll be home at my regular time." She pulled her jacket off the hook, gave her Mom a kiss on the cheek, and ran out the door just as a 'toot' was heard from the front of the house, from Ronnie's best friend, who had come to pick her up.

"Another busy day for the Forrester family," Ginny thought to herself as she went upstairs to get herself ready as well.

CHAPTER TWO

Winter was slow at loosening its grip to spring, but before too long, buds were sprouting on the trees and flowers were showing up in the neighborhood gardens. Carl and his friends had joined with others of their classmates and made a good junior varsity soccer team that competed with many other schools in their county. They won and lost games, as the season progressed, and they had fun in the process, learning some new athletic skills as well.

Spring headed into summer, and at the beginning of May, their school held a Job and Summer Activity Fair sponsored by the Hansonville Chamber of Commerce. This was an opportunity for kids to find summer employment, as well as find out about other activities to fill the short summer months. Hansonville, Vermont, was a popular vacation spot for many city folks who loved the country air and cooler breezes offered by the mountains surrounding this small community. The local town merchants and the Inns in the area were always in need of extra summer help. This was a way for many of the juniors and seniors to earn money for the colleges they would soon be entering. The freshmen and sophomores were no competition there.

Their turn would come in a year or two. For them, there were all sorts of camps on display: sports camps, church camps, scout camps, arts and craft camps, swim camps, and many others- so much for the kids to consider. Carl and his best friends, Tim, Joe, and Tony, were a bit overwhelmed as they sauntered among the booths. Deciding what type of activity they wanted to spend part of their summer doing was the hardest first step. They stopped from time to time and asked questions of the various camp representatives. One by one, the boys dropped off as they stayed to get more information about one camp or another. It seemed that all his friends had found camps that appealed to them-at least at first look-fairly quickly, and it wasn't long before Carl found himself alone. The booth right next to Carl sported a large sign that read: TUCKAWAY RETREAT.

"I wonder what a 'Retreat' is?" he said to himself. "It generally means to 'get away from someplace or something', but how can that be used for a camp? What would you be getting away from? Oh, well! I won't know unless I ask," and he turned to the pleasant-looking young man who appeared to be that booth's representative.

"Hello! My name is Carl Forrester, and I have a question. What do you mean by 'Retreat?'" he said by way of an introduction.

"Nice to meet you, Carl Forrester. I'm Jack Bayland, and that is a very good question."

"Well, I do know the general meaning of retreat- to get away-but a camp is a place you go TO, to have a good time and maybe learn something new." Carl didn't want this man to think he was a complete moron.

"You are absolutely correct: a person retreats to get to someplace better, safer, than where they are at a particular time," Jack continued. "But if you change 'retreat' from a verb-an action, to a noun-a place, it takes on a different meaning. It becomes the better or safer place you want to get to. Does that make sense to you?" Jack looked questioningly at Carl.

Carl thoughtfully pondered what Jack had just said. "Yeaaah, I guess so! I never looked at it that way. So this camp is a place people go to that is better, or safer, than their usual place?" Carl was not quite sure he had it straight yet.

"Well, perhaps not in any dramatic way as we use it. For, us it means a place where kids, and others who may go there, can be where the usual things that fill their lives can be put away for a time, and they can explore different ways of doing and being." Jack was having a little trouble with Carl's question as he had never had to explain 'retreat' before, and he didn't want to insult this boy's daily life.

"Okay! Kids, people go to retreats to get away from their usual lives? How do they do that?" Carl asked, still not clear on this idea of 'retreat'.

"Let me try again!" Jack said. "Let's use your usual routine as an example. What does a usual day in your life look like?"

"Well, right now, I go to school every weekday. Yeah, so I get up by 6:30, and maybe I shower, and maybe I don't, depends. Then I eat breakfast with my Mom and sister-she's a junior." Carl paused a moment. "And then I head to school, meet my friends. We have had soccer these last few weeks, and that's what I do after school. Then it's home, supper, homework, bed, and then get up the next day and do it all over again." He looked expectantly at Jack.

"And I imagine there is some television watching in there as well?" Jack smiled as he posed the question.

"Well, sure, when all the other stuff is done," Carl agreed with a smile of his own.

"I can guarantee that a usual day at the Retreat will be nothing like that," Jack responded. "Let me tell you about the structure of our camp and the kinds of activities we have at the Retreat. We have five units for the kids. Each unit has a cabin for boys and a cabin for girls, with an appropriate counsellor. Each unit has the same number of girls and boys-three to five each, between the ages of fourteen and seventeen. All of the activities are available to all kids who come. We have individual small, and large group things going on all day long. Individual activities are things like arts and crafts, swimming, horseback riding, and archery, to name a few. Small and large group activities include group sports of all kinds, hiking, rock climbing, boating of all types-including canoeing and kayaking, as well as daytrips to nearby points of interest for historical, cultural, entertainment, and recreational purposes. All of our activity options are overseen by folks well-trained and knowledgeable in their chosen areas. Do any of those things interest you, Carl?" Jack finished speaking and looked thoughtfully at the young man.

"Do they? You bet they do!" was Carl's more than enthusiastic reply. "So, what does a kid have to do to go there?"

"Here's our brochure that tells it all," Jack said as he put a colorful packet in Carl's hand. "It's all in there. The most important part is writing a 200-word essay about why you, particularly, want to attend. Take the brochure and show your parents and talk it over. The deadline is coming up in the middle of the month, so don't take too long. Any other questions right now?" Jack looked questioningly at Carl.

Carl looked down at the papers in his hand and slowly shook his head. "No, I can't think of anything else right now. Thanks for taking the time to explain it to me, Mr. Bayland. I'm gonna' go along and look at some of the other things. Maybe I'll see you this summer. Bye!" and Carl gave a small salute, before turning, going on to the next booth, and finally connecting up with his friends.

"Hey, guys, what did you all find?" Carl was the first to ask.

"I had a great talk with some guys who are having a soccer camp over in Newtown. It's gonna' start just after the Fourth. I think that's what I'm doing," Tim spoke up.

"That sounds pretty cool, and then you can show us all how to do better in the fall," Carl said.

"I can't make up my mind between soccer and beginning Junior ROTC," Tony said. "My Dad was in the Army, and he often talks about how much he liked it, but he said it was hard. I'll talk it over with him."

"That's a good idea," Tim agreed.

"What about you, Joe?" Carl asked.

"Well, I'm between working with a group, like Habitat for Humanity, that is going to build some basic houses for new immigrants, or going to swim camp," Joe said. "I think I want to get into the construction field when I finish high school, and building some basic houses would be a good experience," he added. "On the other hand, it might be too much work, and I really like swimming. I guess I've got some thinking to do," he finished and looked around at his friends.

"Yeah, that's a hard choice," Tony sympathized. "Building a house for someone who really needs one could make you feel really good, but it is hard work, and long days. I can see how you really need to think about it," he commiserated with his friend.

"What about you, Carl?" Joe asked.

"I think I'm going to go to this Retreat," and he held up the papers that Jack had given him. "It has a lot of different activities," he continued, and opened the brochure to show his friends pictures of some of them. "It sounds really cool, but I have to talk with my Mom and find out about the money part."

"I'm really glad we came to this Fair," Tim said. "I didn't realize all these things existed."

"Neither did I," Joe seconded. "It's going to be a really fun summer, and we'll have neat stories to tell when school starts in the fall," he enthused as he and all his best friends left the Fair.

"We sure will," Carl nodded in agreement. "Well, I gotta' get home and talk to my Mom. I think you all have some talking to do as well. See you tomorrow," and he was off. He couldn't wait to talk with his Mom and show his sister the brochure of the Retreat.

Only his sister was home when he got there, as it was still just mid- afternoon. "Hey, Sis! Did you get a job lined up for the summer?'

"Yep! I sure did. I'm gonna' be waitressing at the Pancake House. How about that?" she boasted.

"Hey, way to go!" he congratulated her. The Pancake House was known to be one of the very best places to eat any time of the day not just at breakfast time. Word was that the tips were way above the average, and a good waitress could make quite a fortune-at least for a teenager in the summer.

"Yeah! I'm pretty happy about it. It's not far from here and I'll see a lot of my friends. Sally and Martha got hired, too, but I don't think we will always have the same shifts," Veronica continued. "I won't have the same shift every day, either, but that's good 'cause I'll have some mornings to sleep late, and some afternoons to be with the gang, and some evenings free for dating. I couldn't ask for better than that for my last free summer." She gave a deep sigh and plopped down at the kitchen table. "Did you have a good time at the Fair?" she asked Carl as he straddled another chair.

"I did, and I think I have found a camp I would like to go to. I've got some papers about it." He pulled the brochure from his back pocket and dropped it on the table in front of his sister. "Take a look and tell me what you think!"

Veronica took the papers Carl had dropped. She looked them over carefully, reading the text they contained as well. "I like the way they describe the five units, with each unit having two cabins-one for girls and the other for boys. And also that each unit has the same number of girls as boys. It sounds really fun that they do come activities together and some alone, or as part of other groups. And you'll have some free/private time, as well. The activities look terrific." She refolded the brochure and handed it back to her brother.

"Yeah, there sure are enough of them," he agreed. "I can't wait for Mom to get home. The deadline is in just a couple of weeks, and I have to write that paper to go with the application."

"I'm pretty sure Mom will approve," she encouraged with a smile.

"I really hope so, and that it isn't too expensive," Carl replied with a worried look.

"Hey, didn't you read the part about the scholarships they award?" She looked at him in surprise.

Carl was puzzled. "Scholarships? No, where does it say that?" he asked.

Veronica grabbed the brochure out of his hands.

"Give me those papers! Right here, dummy!" and Veronica thumped the papers onto the table, keeping her finger on one particular paragraph. "See! 'Scholarships available'. It says once you are accepted, they send some paperwork to the parents which asks about family finances, and if there may be a problem with the Retreat fee. They make scholarships available to needy families. With only one income in the family, we could be considered 'needy'", she explained.

"No, I didn't read very much in the brochure," Carl admitted. "I had a really nice talk with the guy, Jack something his name was, who was in charge of the booth at the Fair. He told me so much I didn't think of reading the paper. Thanks, Sis!"

"No problem! What are big sisters for anyway?" She ruffled his hair and got up from the table. "I'm gonna' go take a nap. Me, Sally, and Martha are going to a movie tonight. I don't want to fall asleep in the middle of it," she said and headed upstairs to do just that.

"Hey! I thought I was supposed to help you make dinner tonight," he reminded her.

"I know, but I really need a nap," she pleaded. "Mom will understand if I sleep too long, and we can eat later. Okay?"

"Okay! If you are that tired."

"You know? You really are a great brother," she smiled and continued up the stairs.

Carl heard his mother's car roll up the driveway nearly two hours later. He was really anxious to show her the brochure. The more he thought about it, the more excited he got about the Retreat. He hurried to the door and opened it just as his Mom reached the top step. "Hey, Mom. You're finally home." He welcomed her with a big hug.

"Well, that's a welcome I could use every day," she smiled, hugged him back, and stepped into the kitchen. "What's caused all this enthusiasm?"

"Wait til' you hear what I want to do this summer, and Ronnie has some really good news, too. I'll let her tell you herself when she gets up from her nap." Carl relieved his Mom of the bag of groceries she had carried in and set it on the table. "Right now, I have to tell you about the camp place I heard about at the Fair at school today. Sit down and look at this brochure, and there's a lot to read in it too, but I'll tell you all about it first," Carl was tripping over his words as his excitement had them rushing out of his mouth.

"Whoa! Hold up a bit! I'm not going anywhere in the next five minutes. Take a breath, and let me catch mine," Ginny said, gently pushing Carl into a chair and then sitting herself. "Now, what's all this about?"

"Okay…" and for the next ten minutes, Carl told his Mom all he knew about the Retreat. "And here's a brochure that tells all about it as well. I haven't read it all yet," he admitted.

"Give me a few minutes now to look it over and read for myself," she suggested.

Silence prevailed as Ginny carefully read through the information. "Here's something I am very impressed by," she said, and turned the paper for Carl to see what she was referring to. "This is what they are calling 'the camp philosophy'. It says: 'Our philosophy is really quite simple. We want the Retreat to be a place where kids feel safe to be themselves as they share time and experiences with their peers.

Kids in the middle teen years have all sorts of visions and versions of themselves. They have a self-image that may or may not be who they really are. They are conflicted by the way they feel about how they are perceived by others-especially their peers. At the Retreat, there are just a few hard and fast rules: Respect for yourself and others. Be courteous at all times. No bad language. And, of course, there will be no smoking, drinking, or drugs tolerated.' It goes on to say that the parents and kids know these rules right up front, and if they are not adhered to, the teen will be sent home. There will be no refund. I like that," Ginny said, and though she was well aware that Carl could read it by himself, reading it aloud with him was the best way to be sure he heard the message it was meant to convey.

"So, Mom, I think I want to go to Tuckaway this summer. Can we afford it?" he asked hopefully.

"They mention scholarships. We can try for one of those, and then see what else we need to do," she answered. "There's nothing to be lost by trying," she added.

"Then let's do it right now. The application is in here, and if I'm accepted, we'll get the paperwork for the scholarship," he explained. "Jack said that's how it works."

"Sounds good to me," Ginny replied. "So get busy with the essay," she encouraged him, "while I get supper ready."

"On it, Mom!" And both set to work.

CHAPTER THREE

"Hey, slowpoke!" came a shout back down the trail. "Get the lead out and catch up with the rest of us."

"I'm coming, I'm coming!" a young voice answered back.

"Well, hurry up! We're almost at the top, and the view is supposed to be really great. You don't want to miss that!" The voices got more distant.

"I'm hurrying as fast as I can," Lucy, a curly-headed fifteen-year-old girl, whispered to no one. She was having a hard time climbing up the rocky trail. Her legs seemed too short for this uphill trek. This was the first mountain climbing experience she'd had in her fifteen years here on earth, and, at this particular moment, she was wishing that the pleasure could have been postponed indefinitely.

"Here, take my hand," came a voice above her, and a hand appeared over the ledge.

"Oh! Thanks," and she reached up to grab onto it. "I didn't realize a mountain climb would be so hard," she managed to wheeze out. With the aid of the helping hand, Lucy clambered up the sloping stretch of mountain trail. "I think I'd like to stop for a minute," she said. "I need to catch my breath."

"Sure thing! Take your time. The view isn't going anywhere anytime soon. I'm Carl, by the way. We met briefly at dinner last night. I'm one of the three guys in Unit three," Carl said as he sank to the ground beside Lucy.

"Yes, I remember meeting all of you, but I didn't remember who was who. So, you're Carl. I'll remember that now. The other two were Harry and Zach, right?" she questioned.

"Yep! Harry's the one with red hair and freckles. He's seventeen. Zack's the dark-haired, short guy, and he's fifteen like me," Carl answered.

"Well, nice to meet you again, and thanks for the help. We better get up there with the others," Lucy suggested as she rose, brushed off the seat of her jeans, adjusted the straps of her backpack, and turned up the trail.

"Right!" Carl agreed and set off behind her. "It's not that much farther."

And it wasn't. The going also wasn't as difficult as it had been. The mountain had begun to level off as it neared its top. In no time at all, they spotted the rest of their Unit Three group gathered together on the mountain's crest, apparently admiring the open view and the valley below.

"Hurrah! We made it," Carl called out.

"We were about to send out a search party," seventeen-year-old June said as she pushed her wind-blown, light brown ponytail out of her eyes, turned to them, and beckoned. "Come see this view! It's really something, and you can see the lake and the Retreat way over to the left.

Carl and Lucy slipped their packs off on the pile of the others and hurried to join the group. Shelley motioned Lucy to her side. "I was getting worried about you," she said. "Are you okay?"

"Yeah! I just got really tired and needed a rest. I've never done anything like this before. Some days, the most exercise I get is turning the pages of a good book," she replied.

The girls shared a brief hug. This was only their second day at the Retreat, but they had clicked right away, even though dark-haired Shelley was a year older than Lucy. They lived in the same city, but had never met. They were having fun comparing notes on places they had been and things they had done at home, and found they had a lot in common. Lucy was an only child, and Shelley seemed like a big sister.

"Wow!" Lucy exclaimed as she gazed out over the valley. "It seems like you can see forever. The sky looks so big. And the land is so green and full of trees." There was wonder in her voice. "And look at the river flowing through it all!"

"Yes, that river flows into the lake at the Retreat," Hank Martin, counsellor for the boys' half of Unit Three, told them all. "And then out the other side. We can do some canoeing someday. It's a really fun activity, isn't it, Ms. C?" He looked at the counsellor for the Unit Three girls for confirmation.

"It truly is," Beth Challace affirmed. "Canoeing is one of my most favorite things to do. Of course, you will need some careful instruction before we go out on the river. We can set a time to do that this week. How does that sound?"

"Great! How about tomorrow?" Harry enthusiastically shouted out.

"Yeah!" Shelley and Zack spoke at the same time.

"Whoa!" Mr. Hank cautioned. "We have to check when the waterfront crew has an opening in their schedule for the instruction. We can do that as soon as we get back today, okay?"

"Okay, let's hope we can do that real soon," Harry said. "I'm really looking forward to getting into a canoe."

"And so am I!" Shelley excitedly agreed.

"So, now that's settled, let's find some comfortable rocks where we can sit and have our lunch." Ms. C suggested.

"Yeah! I was wondering when we were going to get to that," Zach piped up. "I'm starving!"

"Alright! Let's eat!"

Backpacks were sorted out. Lunches were pulled out, and silence descended for a short time as the hungry hikers settled down to eat the box lunches the kitchen crew at the Retreat had provided for them. It was also a good opportunity to regain some energy for the trip back down the trail. While going down was certainly easier than climbing up, it was also a bit more dangerous as rocks had a bad habit of rolling under unwary feet, and sending a hiker into a nasty twisted ankle, or a headlong fall.

"Everybody finished?" Mr. Hank called out a half hour later.

Affirmatives were heard all around.

"Then let's head back down. Please be very careful. Watch every step, and be aware of loose rocks. If you see something that doesn't look safe, warn the people near you. Don't go off the marked trail. Be sure you can always see another person," were his parting words as the group moved behind him and headed down the mountainside. Ms. Challace brought up the rear.

"This has been a truly awesome day," Lucy confided to Carl, who was following her in line.

"Yes, it has, hasn't it?" he agreed. "And our two weeks are just beginning. We are going to have a great time."

There was little conversation as everyone was paying good attention to the downward trail. Mr. Hank called a rest after about forty-five minutes. "Okay, everyone, taking a few swigs from your canteens. Don't want to get dehydrated."

Carl and Lucy shared a rock. Carl was looking at all the mountains surrounding them. He was fascinated by their size and variety of trees and plants. Suddenly, he stood up and fixed his gaze on one particular spot across the valley.

"What are you looking at?" Lucy asked and stood up beside him.

"I'm looking at that dark spot on that mountain."

"Which mountain?" Lucy questioned.

"That one is directly across from us. Can you see that dark spot just there in the middle? There's an especially big rock next to it," and he raised his arm to point.

"Nooo, oh, yes, I see it now," Lucy said. "What about the dark spot?"

"I'm wondering if there might be a cave behind there," he replied. "Mr. Hank, can you come here a minute?" he called out loudly.

"Be right there!" And Hank made his way back up the short stretch of trail that separated them. "What's up?" he inquired.

"Are there any caves in these mountains?" Carl asked.

"It's a pretty sure thing that wherever there are mountains, there are going to be caves," he replied. "Why do you ask?"

"Look over there at that mountainside. Do you see that dark spot beside that large boulder sticking out?" Carl raised his arm and pointed again.

Mr. Hank squinted his eyes and looked to where Carl was indicating. "Yeah! I see the spot you mean. That is Mount Gregory. From here, it is hard to tell very much, but I know there is a trail somewhere in that area. Maybe we could take a hike over and check it out one day this week."

"That would be great," Carl exclaimed. "Hey, Harry, Zach, come here and take a look."

"What's all the racket about?" Harry called back.

"Come up here and see for yourself," he said, beckoning the two boys to hurry up.

When the boys reached them, Carl again pointed across the valley. "Can you see that dark spot over there?" he asked.

"Where?" Harry quizzically searched the opposite mountainside with his eyes.

"What are you talking about? I don't see anything special?" was Zach's comment.

"Well, if you look closely, you can see a dark spot among the trees, next to that really huge rock," Carl prompted.

"Okaaaaaay, I see something dark over there," Harry agreed. "What about it?"

"I'm wondering if it might be a cave. Wouldn't it be fun to explore a cave?" he added. "Mr. Hank said there is a trail over there near that spot, and maybe we could go over there one day this week. Are you guys up for that?" he asked anxiously.

"Sure!" Harry said with a big grin. "That sounds like a fine adventure."

"Weelll, I don't know about that!" Zack said dubiously. "Don't caves have bats in them, and monstrous spiders?"

"You've been watching too many horror movies, Zack," Lucy, who had been standing quietly to the side, teased him.

"You mean you would be very happy to go crawling around in a cave?" Miss Smarty Pants," he challenged.

"Well, I don't think I would use the word 'happy', but I think it would be interesting to at least investigate it," she replied with a smile.

By this time, Ms. C, Shelley, and June had come up to the rest of the group and were also looking across the valley at this mysterious spot, which may-or may not-indicate the presence of a cave.

"It would definitely be worth a day trip to find out for ourselves," Ms. C said, offering her opinion.

"I've never seen a real cave," June said. "I'm with Zack in being a little leery of what we might meet inside a cave."

"Okay, I think we are getting a little ahead of ourselves here," Mr. Hank interrupted all the chatter. "First of all, we don't even know for sure if there is a cave over there. Maybe it's just a mass of boulders sort of hiding behind the trees. Even if it is a cave, no one has to go inside if they don't want to. And it's not like we are going to head over there this minute. So, let's all calm down and safely finish today's outing. Let's get going! Ready, gang?"

"Yep!"

"I'm ready!"

"Sure thing!" voices came from all sides.

Mr. Hank took his place at the front of the line, and the rest stepped into file behind him, with Ms. C back at the end.

The trail was too narrow for hikers to walk side by side. It was a single file most of the way down. Because of the twists and turns of the trails and the mountain greenery, Ms. C did not always have a good view of all the kids, but she was always close enough to hear them. Mr. Hank, at the front, could alert them of any possible hazards and guide them over or around them. Nonetheless, she was surprised when she heard the deep rumble of falling rocks and cries of surprise and pain ahead of her. She could see June and Harry look at each other and then begin to hurry along the trail. She quickly took pursuit, calling out, "What's happened? I'm coming!"

"Oh, my gosh! I hope no one is hurt," she was muttering to herself as she hurried along. It seemed like forever, but it was only minutes before she could see the kids huddled together, obviously at the scene of the trouble.

"Okay, kids, I'm here. Move over! Let me see what needs to be done," she said as she moved forward.

"It's Lucy, Ms. C." Shelley cried a bit hysterically. "She just slipped, and the next thing, the side of the trail just collapsed. And, and, and….she disappeared." Shelly was crying so hard now that her words became incoherent.

Ms. C quickly took charge. "Okay, kids! Move back up the trail. We don't want anyone else to take a tumble. Find a good place and sit down."

Just at that moment, Ms. C saw Mr. Hank appear, coming back up the trail at a good clip, with Zack and Harry right behind him. "We heard the rumble and cries….Oh!"…. and he stopped dead. "Hold up, boys!" he said and spread his arms to hold them back. "Are you all okay up there?" he called to Ms. C.

"Yes, June, Carl, and Shelley are safe and here with me. Can you see Lucy from where you are?" she asked anxiously, pausing to take a breath. "Shelley said 'she disappeared' when the side of the trail collapsed."

"Okay, everyone, very carefully find a place to sit. I don't know what made this section of the trail give way, but we don't want any more of it to do that," Mr. Hank directed. From his position further down the mountain, he could see Lucy slumped in a pile of dirt and rubble under a bush that appeared to have stopped her fall. "I can see Lucy," he called up to Ms. C. "I'm going to go to her."

Slowly and carefully, Mr. Hank made his way through the underbrush to Lucy's side. Some small rocks and dirt spilled down on them as he gently touched Lucy's arm. "Lucy, can you hear me?"

"Uh! Huh! What…what happened?" Lucy stuttered. She opened her eyes and tried to sit up.

"No, Lucy, stay still. You have had a fall. Where does it hurt? Can you move your arms and legs?" Mr. Hank asked.

"I thin…think so," and she lifted her left arm. "That feels okay." But when she moved her right arm, she winced in pain. "That one doesn't feel so good," she said, holding back tears. In the meantime, Mr. Hank had been inspecting her pant legs for rips and signs of blood. Visually, things looked good.

"Let's see if you can stand up," he suggested as he moved around her to support her on the left. Very slowly, Lucy rose to her feet. She wobbled and leaned into Mr. Hank. "That's good, Lucy," he encouraged. "Okay, now put all your weight on your left foot." Lucy did so with no evidence of discomfort.

"Now, on your right foot," he instructed.

"Ouch! That hurts," she whimpered.

"Where is the pain?" he asked

"Down around my ankle," she said. "I can't put it down," and tears slid over her cheeks.

"Okay! Let's just sit still for a moment," Mr. Hank advised, and he eased her slowly back to the ground. He gently lifted Lucy's right foot and raised the bottom of her pant leg to get a look at the ankle. There was no broken skin. But above her shoe top, he could see some swelling. From the small first aid kit he had in his backpack, he took a roll of thick, white cloth.

"I'm going to wrap this strip of cloth over your shoe and around your ankle to give your ankle more support for now, okay?" he explained to Lucy.

Lucy bravely tried to smile and nodded. "Okay!"

"Ms. C.?" he called up to the trail. "You need to change places with me. Can you come down here safely?"

"I'm on my way," she called back, and was soon at his side.

"I need to go to the Retreat for help. We need a stretcher. I'll take the rest of the kids with me," he told her. "Lucy seems to have a sprained ankle and a sore right arm. You need to stay here with her."

"Okay! We'll be fine," she smiled at Lucy. "Won't we?"

Lucy managed a small smile of her own. "Yes, I'm sure we will be, Ms. C."

Mr. Hank rose and scrambled up the trail to where the rest of the kids had been sitting in anxious silence. "Harry, do you think you will be able to guide medical help back here?"

"Yes, I'm sure I can," Harry readily accepted the responsibility.

"Great! Now, kids," Mr. Hank looked at them one by one, "let's get going. We need to be as quick as safely possible. We have some good daylight hours left, and Ms. C and Lucy will be fine until Harry can get back here with the proper help."

Ms. C and Lucy could hear the rest of the group making their way around the break in the trail. Soon, there were no more sounds; the forest was still.

"Are you in much pain, Lucy?" Ms. C asked softly, worried about Lucy's comfort.

"As long as I don't move, I'm all right," she answered.

"I'm very glad the day is a warm one," Ms. C continued.

"Me, too. The forest really is a beautiful place," Lucy added. "This is the first time I have ever been in such a lovely place. I have seen pictures in books and magazines, but I never imagined how wonderful it really is to be among all these big trees and so much green. It's magical!"

"Yes, I think so, too," Ms. C agreed. "Are there any parks near where you live?"

"Well, there is a place we call a park, but it is mostly for little kids. It has some swings and a seesaw and a merry-go-round, you know, the kind where the kids push it around and then jump on? And there are some benches and a couple of paths in and out. Old people often sit on the benches and watch the little kids have fun. Sometimes, at night when the little kids are in bed, me and my friends go and play around a bit, and just hang out, talk, that kinda stuff." Lucy lapsed into silence, suddenly feeling shy that she had chattered so much.

"That sounds like a nice place for everyone in the neighborhood," Ms. C. commented. "We had a place like that in the neighborhood where I grew up, too. Everyone would gather there for special days like Memorial Day and the Fourth of July. Everyone would bring food. We'd have a picnic and play some games. It was always a fun time."

"Where did you grow up, Ms. C?" Lucy asked.

"In Boston," she replied.

"Oh, that's a very historical place, isn't it?" Lucy was very interested in hearing about Boston. "My parents often talk about Boston. They met there when both of them were in college. I really want to go there sometime. Can you tell me about it?" Lucy was excited, and her injuries faded away as Ms. C began to talk.

"Yes, certainly Boston is a very historical place, especially for the Revolutionary War. You have most likely studied that in history class?" she looked questioningly at Lucy.

"Oh! Yes! And I loved hearing about those times. The people seemed so brave and determined," she eagerly replied.

"You're right. They were determined to get out from under the rule of the king. America would have no king telling them what to do, and taxing them so hard," she continued. "When you go to Boston, one of the things you really must do is take a walk along the Freedom

Trail. It is a marked trail through the city, taking you from one historical location to another. There is the Old South Church where political meetings took place, and where the Liberty Boys departed from for their attack on the ship, 'Little Beaver", and the Boston Tea Party. Then there is Paul Revere's house in the North End, near the Old North Church, where the lights were hung to warn the Minute Men of Concord and Lexington of the movements of the British soldiers." Ms. C. was getting caught up in the story she was telling a very attentive Lucy. Aches and pains were forgotten as the forest was transformed into the old city streets of Boston.

Meanwhile, Mr. Hank had been carefully hurrying the rest of the kids along the trail back to the Retreat and getting help for Lucy. "We're nearly there he called out. Harry, go on ahead and let Mr. Matt (the top man at the Retreat) know we are coming, and we will need a medical team to go up the trail with proper equipment for an injured hiker."

"I'm on it," Harry called back. And, as the trail had leveled off, he began to jog and was soon out of sight.

Shortly after that, Mr. Hank, June, Shelley, Carl, and Zack arrived as well. Already, they could see that the EMTs were there, packing the things they would need for this rescue mission into large backpacks. A collapsible stretcher was there as well. Harry was standing and talking with Matt and one of the EMTs. Hank immediately went over to them.

"Ms. C has stayed with the injured girl. Her name is Lucy Clark. She was alert and talking when we left. There doesn't seem to be any head injury, but you will need the stretcher as her right ankle is badly swollen," and he explained the situation.

"That's important information," EMT Bob Bryant thanked him. "It's good to know what we can expect when we get there."

"This young man," and EMT Marian Wyman indicated Harry, "said he would lead us back up the trail, "so let's get started," she urged. "The day is getting shorter by the minute."

"Right! Lead on, Harry", EMT Bryant pointed up the trail, and they were off, Harry leading at a good pace.

Ms. C had just finished telling of the 'Shot heard round the world', when she and Lucy became aware of the sound of voices coming up the trail. "I think our rescuers are just about here," she said to Lucy. "That was really fast, wasn't it?"

"The time has flown, it seems," Lucy agreed, and they both looked up at the trail above them just as Harry's smiling face appeared.

"Help is here," he announced. "EMTs Bryant and Wyman," he introduced them as they began to cautiously make their way down the unstable slope.

"You made really good time, Harry," Ms. C said. She moved aside as EMT Wyman slid the last few inches down next to Lucy's side.

"I'm EMT Wyman. How are you feeling Lucy?" Marian asked. She reached out to hold Lucy's wrist to check her pulse.

"I'm feeling pretty good. My right arm and leg don't feel so good, but the rest of me seems okay," Lucy answered. She even had a smile for the EMTs.

"Okay! That's all good," EMT Bryant smiled right back at her, and gently lifted her leg to check her ankle. "This wrap on your ankle has done a good job to help keep the swelling down," he said. "Now, for that arm. Because we don't know just what has happened to it, I think we need to put it in a sling to keep it as quiet as possible. How does that sound?" he asked.

"Like a good idea," Lucy responded. She tried to sit up a little straighter.

"Hold on there, Lucy. Let me get the sling ready, and we'll do this slowly and carefully."

He gently slid one end of the sling around Lucy's neck and pulled it to the other side. He laid the sling over her arm which lay across her waist. He took the other end and slowly worked it up between her arm and body until the other end reached just above her shoulder. Then he tied the two ends together.

"There now! How does that feel?" he asked.

"I hardly felt you doing that," Lucy said in amazement. "It feels fine. Thank you!" She really did feel better now that help was there, though the waiting time had passed so quickly listening to Ms. C. and her stories of Boston.

EMT Bryant pulled the stretcher from his pack and soon had it firmly put together. "Okay, young lady, we're going to help get you secured to this portable bed here, and then we'll be able to carry you fairly comfortably down the rest of this mountain. What do you say?"

"Let's do it! I'm ready," Lucy bravely agreed, though getting settled on that stretcher wasn't pain-free.

Luckily, there was still some fading daylight left as the small group slowly came down the final stretch of the trail into the Retreat. And what a fine welcome they received as Lucy was conveyed to the nurse's station, where she was transferred to a proper bed and the attention of the very capable Nurse Kathy, who was on duty.

CHAPTER FOUR

"**R**ise and shine!" Ms. C cheerfully called out, just as the Dining Hall gong announced the start of a new day with breakfast ready for the hungry campers. June rolled over, opened her eyes and smiled at Ms. C.

"Good Morning," she said. "I'm hungry!"

Shelley groaned, "Do I have to get up? Really?" she complained.

"Com'on, no sleepy heads allowed in the Dining Hall," Ms. C. encouraged her. "Last one to breakfast has to wash the dishes. You don't want to do that, do you?" she kidded.

"Okay, okay, I'm up," and Shelley swung her feet to the floor. "I wonder how Lucy's doing this morning," she said as she looked up at Ms. C.

"Mr. Matt will probably have a report for us this morning," she replied. "If he doesn't have one, we can go over to the infirmary and find out for ourselves."

"Just give me a minute and I'll be ready," Shelley assured her. "Morning', June," she said through a big yawn.

"Right back at ya," June said. She was nearly out the door. "I'll go ahead and get us a spot."

"We'll be right along, June. Find a spot for the boys, too, okay?" she added.

"Will do!" and she was gone.

"Are you ready, slowpoke?" Ms. C. queried.

"Yep, see!" Shelley struck a 'ta-da' pose.

"Okay! Lead the way!" and Ms. C. held the door open.

The Dining Hall was a very short walk through the trees surrounding Unit Three's position on the Retreat's site on the lake shore. The entire site was quite beautiful. All five Units were situated in stands of trees which formed a semicircle around the main entrance, administration building, bath house, and the waterfront. Behind the Units were sports fields, the stables, and the archery and rifle ranges. Well-maintained foot trails led between all the various areas. It was a nearly perfect place for a summer camp, and the campers always loved being there even those who were homesick at first soon came to see the wonder of this special place.

It didn't take Ms. C. and Shelley very long to join June, Mr. Hank. Carl, Harry, and Zack in the Dining Hall. "Good Morning, all," Ms. C. greeted them.

"Morning, yourself, and welcome," Mr. Hank answered. "Let's eat and get this day underway."

"Right on," Carl agreed. "Let's get in line before all the good stuff is gone," and he got up from the table to lead the way.

When everyone had filled their plates and were seated again at the table, Ms. C. asked, "So, who's doing what today?"

"Can I get some swimming lessons at the lake?" Shelley asked.

"You can't swim?" Zack said, incredulously.

"Zack, that's not a very nice way to ask," Mr. Hank admonished. "Try again!"

"I'm just surprised that someone in their teens hasn't learned to swim. That's all!" Zack replied. "Where I live the school has swimming as part of the Phys. Ed. Program. Sorry, Shelley!" He was embarrassed.

"That's okay, Zack. I know you didn't mean anything by it. But, no, I can't swim. My school doesn't have that kind of program, and if you want to learn to swim, you have to sign up at the YWCA, and it costs a lot of money, at least for my family," Shelley explained.

"Yes, Shelley, to answer your question Two, you can get swimming lessons at the waterfront," Ms. C. said. "The instructor is Ms. Lanier. She is very qualified, having swum in competition in the last Olympics. You'll like her a lot. She is very patient and sensitive to new learners," she continued. "I'll go with you and introduce you if you'd like."

"I think I can do that myself, Ms. C., but thanks for the offer," Shelley smiled at her. "I'm a little nervous, but excited to learn."

"I think I'm going to go for photography today," Carl spoke up. "I have seen some really great photos that some kids at my school have taken. If I can learn about some of the techniques, I'd love to get myself a good camera and maybe think of a career in that field."

"Well, now would be a very good time to get started, Carl. You can take all the time you want practicing," Mr. Hank assured him. "Go for it!"

"I'm going to arts and crafts," June announced. "My aunt Nancy paints beautiful pictures of flowers and trees. She says she finds it very soothing and quiets her soul. I know that sounds kinda weird, but that's what she says, and if that's how it makes her feel, it must be a pretty good hobby, and I'm ready to try it," she finished.

""That's a fine idea," Ms. C. said. "What about you, Harry?"

"I'm going down to the woodworking shop. I've done a little of that at school, and I'd like to learn more," Harry replied firmly. "You want to come with me, Zack?" he looked at him as he asked.

"Yeah, I guess so. I haven't thought of anything else," Zack answered. He didn't sound very enthusiastic, but Harry didn't mind that. He knew Zack would enjoy it once they were there.

"Okay," Mr. Hank looked around the table at the mostly-happy faces. "It sounds like everyone is going to have interesting and rewarding mornings. I look forward to hearing your results at lunchtime. Ms. C and I are going to check up on Lucy and will have news for you as well. See you all then."

"Okays!" and "See ya's!" sounded around the table as everyone got up to go to his or her own chosen activity.

"Let's get over to the infirmary and see our patient," Mr. Hank said to Ms. C., who was anxious to find out how Lucy was doing and what could be expected of her. She hoped she would not have to go home. Lucy was a very enthusiastic camper and had been having a wonderful time. She would be very disappointed to have to leave.

"Yes, let's before any more time goes by," and she practically pulled Mr. Hank along.

They were very pleased to see Lucy sitting up in bed with a bright smile on her face.

"Good morning," she happily called out. "The nurse has good news."

"Indeed, I do," Nurse Kathy said from behind them. "Miss Lucy just has a twisted ankle. She should be able to use it quite well after another day of rest." Nurse Kathy was now standing in front of them beside Lucy's bed. "She has a bruised shoulder, and that also should be less painful and troublesome after a day of bed rest. There will be a few gentle exercises she will learn to do to get it back to full use. The X-rays have shown no serious damage. We have talked with her parents and they are agreeable that she can stay here, as long as she is a good patient for the next day," she smiled at Lucy.

"Oh! You better believe that I will be the best patient you've ever had," she promised. "I really, really don't want to go home. I am having the best time ever, even if I did fall down a mountain. It will be a good story to tell the kids at school, about how I had to get rescued off a big mountain."

"Well, don't make it sound too scary or other kids from your school might not want to come here," Ms. C. cautioned.

"Yeah, we don't want them to get the idea that this is a dangerous place," Mr. Hank added.

"Oh, no! I wouldn't want that. In fact, I'm going to tell them all to fill out the application. I just want it to sound a bit dramatic- you know, just enough to make them jealous that I had such a romantic experience," Lucy gave them an impish grin.

"I think we have a budding actress here," Ms. C. commented to Mr. Hank. "I think for now you should just focus on getting better, and do just exactly what Nurse Kathy tells you, okay? Right?"

"You bet!" and Lucy slapped palms with Mr. Hank.

"We'll tell the others how you are doing, and I'm sure some of them may come to see you for themselves," Ms. C. added, as she and Mr. Hank turned and left.

"See ya' real soon! Tell the gang I'm doing great and will be back before they get a chance to miss me," Lucy called out in parting.

"We sure will," Mr. Hank promised.

Ms. C. and Mr. Hank walked to the administration building together, then went their separate ways to tend to the never-ending paperwork that was part of their jobs. But first, Ms. C. made a call to Lucy's parents to assure them that Lucy was doing well and was, in no way, wanting or ready to go home.

Lunch time arrived on schedule, and soon all the kids were back in the Dining Hall.

"Before we do anything else, we want to let you know that Lucy is doing very well after her accident yesterday," Ms. C. announced. "She doesn't have to go home, as her injuries are minor and will only require a day or two of rest, right here in our infirmary. There is nothing broken, and she says she really isn't in much pain-for which we are very grateful," she finished with a big smile.

""That's the best news ever!" Carl said

"Oh, my goodness," Shelley said. "I think I am going to cry from happiness," and she did dab at her eyes.

"Great!" "That's the best news!" "Wonderful!" and "Super"! came from the rest of the gang.

"Well, now that that's settled, how did everyone's morning go?" Mr. Hank asked.

"Super!" Shelley sang out. "I didn't drown, and now I can float and do a good doggie paddle. That's fine progress Ms. Lanier told me. I know I'll do better next lesson." She was obviously very pleased with her morning lesson.

"Wow! A doggie paddler already." Ms. C. gave Lucy's shoulders a brief hug. "Good for you!"

"And how was your morning, Carl?" Mr. Hank asked, turning to him.

"Yeah! Okay!" he replied a bit nervously. "So, I really enjoyed talking with Mr. Luke, who's the photography guy here," Carl continued. "Now I at least understand how a camera works, and what all the different settings are about. There was even time for me to take a few photos. Mr. Luke said he would develop them, and they would be ready tomorrow. I'm really excited about seeing them," he continued as he took his place at the table.

"I think we would all like to see them, Carl," Mr. Hank said encouragingly. "What did you photograph?"

"Uh! The topic wasn't very interesting 'cause I was just practicing," he began. "There's an old tree stump at the edge of the woods near the photography shed, and there are some purple and white wild flowers around it. I took a couple pictures of that from different angles, that's all," he explained.

"That sounds like it would make a very pretty picture," Shelley said, and smiled at him.

"That sounds like something I would like to paint," June spoke up. "Maybe you can show me that spot, Carl? I had a wonderful morning learning how to use a palette, and mix colors to get the exact color I want. The instructor, Ms. Darcy, had set out a bowl of artificial fruit for us to practice on. It had a lot of different colors, and I truly enjoyed the experience-and the challenge-of seeing how close I could make my painting to the example. Ms. Darcy complemented my effort, and said she thought I could get to be a fine artist. That made me feel good," she finished.

"And we also look forward to seeing your picture," Ms. C. said. "Did you bring it?"

"No! Not today. It wasn't dry enough for me to bring it with me," June said. "I can probably get it tomorrow, or the next time I go."

"Okay! Well, we'll just have to be patient 'til then, won't we, kids?" Mr. Hank said. "And how did the woodworking go?" he asked, as he turned to Harry and Zack sitting at the end of the table.

The two boys looked at each other. "You go!" Harry told Zack.

"Not me! I'm no public speaker," Zack said brusquely. "You go right ahead."

"Alright! But there's no reason to be bashful now. You sure did your share of the talking at the class, acting like you knew what all the tools were for," Harry said, scowling at Zack.

Zack scowled right back at him, but stubbornly kept his mouth shut.

"Okay guys, let's keep it friendly," Mr. Hank admonished

"So, Mr. Jack was the teacher," Harry began, after giving Zack another black look. "He told us his father and grandfather had both been carpenters and cabinetmakers. Carpenters make structures like houses and garages, and cabinetmakers make fine furniture. Mr. Jack's father and grandfather did both." Harry paused and looked around to see if everyone was listening. "Well, we didn't think we were going to build a house-and Mr. Jack agreed on that." There was laughter at that. "Yeah! So, he showed us pictures of some small things we could make using different tools. A picture frame was one of them-maybe for your picture, June?"

"Sounds good to me," June grinned and nodded.

"So, anyway," Harry continued, "we could also make a trinket box, a cutting board, a yard ornament-and he had a bunch of designs for those-even a tool box. I'm making a tool box for myself. You can tell them what you're making yourself, Zack," and Harry just stopped talking.

"Uh, well," a pink flush colored Zack's cheeks.

"Com'on Zack, we're all friends here," Shelley spoke up. "What are you afraid of? We won't bite! I promise! And we won't even laugh-at least not any more than we are now." And she gave him a big smile of encouragement.

"Uh, uh! Well, I haven't completely decided," Zack stuttered a bit. "I'm thinking I want to make a yard ornament for my Mom's flower garden, but there are so many designs that I'm having a hard time deciding." And he was done.

"Now, that wasn't so hard, was it?" Shelley teased.

Zack didn't respond, but the color faded from his cheeks and he visibly relaxed,

"Let's eat, group," Ms. C suggested. "This afternoon we are going to challenge Unit Five to a game at the sport field."

Lunch was finished in about forty-five minutes and Unit Three headed to the sport field. Before lunch, Mr. Hank had spoken with Joey Davis, counselor for the boys in Unit Five, and they were all there when they arrived. However, Unit Five had eight kids, while they were down to five, with the temporary loss of Lucy.

"How about we borrow one of your girls?" Ms. C. suggested to Rebecca May, the girl's counselor.

"I'll volunteer," Martha offered, even before Rebecca had time to ask them. Martha and June had met at Arts and Crafts that morning, and had really enjoyed their time together.

"Well, thank you very much," Ms. C said. "Welcome to our group-just temporarily, of course," and she smiled her welcome.

"Yeah, we won't beat your group too badly," Zack promised.

A very lively game of volleyball ensued. The teams were pretty evenly matched, and at the end of the game, the score was tied.

"Great game," Mr. Hank announced as the groups lined up for the parting hand slap.

"Unit three, let's head back to our cabin area," Ms. C announced. "It would be a good idea to make some plans for the next few days, and then there will be private time until supper. Sound like a plan?" she finished.

"Yeah!" "Okay!" "Sure thing!" greeted her idea.

In no time the kids, with Mr. Hank and Ms. C., were seated on logs and rocks around the empty campfire circle where there would be a fire, later in the evening.

"Okay," Mr. Hank began. "Tomorrow there is going to be a whole Retreat trip to a recreated settler's village about twenty miles from here. There are replicas of buildings and other structures from the early days of the settling and building of the village. There are people dressed in the style of those days, doing the chores and tasks necessary for life then. Others will be demonstrating some special skills, such as barrel making and spinning wool. Not only will they tell you and show you, but you will be able to try some of those things for yourself."

"It's a very interesting place to visit," Ms. C. assured them. "There are farm animals that you can pet, and even hold if you would like to. You may also be asked to help at some of the demonstrations."

"Wow! That sounds like wicked fun," Shelley enthused. "What time are we going?"

"We'll be leaving right after breakfast," Ms. C. replied.

"What about Lucy?" Carl asked. "Will she be able to come, too?"

"That's very thoughtful of you to think of her, Carl," Mr. Hank said. "I'm sure the infirmary has a wheelchair we can use."

"Yeah, and we can take turns pushing her," Harry offered.

"Speak for yourself," Zack said.

"Don't be so mean, Zack," June frowned at him. "How would you like it if you were the one that was injured, and got left out of the fun activities?"

"Sorry, sorry! I didn't mean anything." Zack lowered his head and scuffed at the ground with his sneaker, color rising in his cheeks-again. He just couldn't seem to fit in with these kids. He was always saying, or doing something that got him criticism from someone. Maybe he should just call his Mom to come and get him. Since his father had become a very angry and unpleasant man since he lost his job last year, and turned to drinking, he and his Mom had gotten real close. She'd be glad to see him.

"That's okay, Zack. I know you will help if you are needed," Shelley consoled him, and gave him a smile, which he saw only out of the corner of his eye from his lowered head. It did make him feel a little bit better, though.

"Any questions?" Mr. Hank asked, and looked around at all the kids.

"How long are we staying there?" June asked.

"I think the plan is to be there until after lunch," Ms. C. answered. "The Dining Hall is packing bag lunches for all of us. There is a fine picnic area at the village, so we can eat there, and even stay after that if there are still things everyone would like to see."

"I'm really looking forward to tomorrow," Harry said.

"Me, too," echoed June. "I have read stories of those times, and it will be great to see some of the things I have only read about."

"I hope there are a lot of baby animals we can hold," Shelley said with a wistful look on her face.

"I think there is a very good chance of that," Mr. Hank assured her. "Farms are great places to find baby animals of all kinds. Just remember, we can't bring any of them back with us."

That got a lot of laughter from the kids. "Okay! Private time 'til supper," Ms. C. reminded them, as she stood up. "I'll be in the administration building if anyone is looking for me. See you all at supper," she added as she headed up the wooded trail.

"Okay, guys and gals, you are on your own for a while," Mr. Hank said. "I have a few things to do as well. Enjoy the rest of your afternoon!"

"See ya' later!" "Bye for now!" "'Til supper, Mr. Hank," the kids returned his parting comments.

"Hey, guys, want to go to the infirmary with me and tell Lucy about tomorrow?" Shelley invited.

"Sure!" "Good Idea!" "Let's go!" and the group set out.

It took less than five minutes for them to arrive at the infirmary.

"Where's Lucy?" they asked in one voice, eager to see their missing group member.

"Hold up there! Not so loud! This is a place for ailing folks, you know," came a warning voice just inside the door.

"Sorry!" June answered in a softer voice. "We're just excited to see Lucy and tell her about tomorrow. Where is she?"

Nurse Kathy appeared from the nurse's office. "If you'll quietly follow me, we will go find her. I think she is just where I left her an hour or so ago reading a book. Let's see! Why, 'yes' just as I suspected!" Nurse Kathy grinned at them, "Ta-da! Don't stay too long as Lucy is still under 'rest' orders, and that means peace and quiet. Okay?"

"Okay!" the kids chorused, and Nurse Kathy left them to their visit.

Lucy was sitting up in bed, and an open book lay on the covers beside her. The kids were glad she wasn't napping. "Hey, you guys! I've been hoping you'd come by and see me. What have you all been doing?" Everyone started talking at once. "Wait! Slow down! I can't understand any of you," Lucy complained.

"Okay, okay!" Shelley put out her hands to shush the others. "Let me talk first, all right?"

"You don't have to be bossy about it," Zack said grudgingly.

"Sorry, but me and Lucy are buddies......"

"Hey, we are all buddies here, aren't we?" Carl interrupted.

"Well, of course we are," Shelley agreed. "But me and Lucy have become special buddies these last couple days, and...."

"Okay, okay you've made your point. The floor is yours," and Zack gave a brief bow and a swish of his hand.

After a brief look at Zack to assure herself that he really was done interrupting, Shelley began again. "Well, the most exciting thing is that the whole Retreat is going on a field trip tomorrow to a historical old-fashioned village a ways from here and........"

"But what about me?" Lucy wailed.

"That's the most exciting thing about it. You are going to go, too, and there is a wheelchair here and you are going to be personally pushed around by these strong, young gentlemen, our partners in Unit Three," Shelley finished explaining, grinning from ear to ear. "Isn't that just the best thing ever?"

"Wow! That sure is! And you three gallant guys are going to be my personal drivers?" Lucy queried skeptically.

"At your service, m' lady," Carl said. "We'll take turns."

"I'm still thinking about it," Zack said.

"Oh, don't pay any attention to him," June said. "He's mostly bark and no bite. I'm sure he'll help if it's needed, won't you Zack?"

"Probably, but don't hold me to it," Zack answered.

"I'm sure we will manage just fine, Lucy," Harry assured her. "The village has a lot of things to see and do, and even animals we can pet. So I'm sure we will have a really great time."

"Okay, kids, that's all for today. Little Miss Lucy still needs her rest," Nurse Kathy, announced as she appeared in the doorway. "I understand tomorrow in going to be a big day, so it's all the more important for her to start the day refreshed and ready. Out you go!" and they were hustled out of the room.

"That sure was the bums rush!" Zack commented as they stood outside the infirmary.

"Yeah, but Lucy really does need to feel good tomorrow to enjoy the trip, and not get too tired, or be in too much pain," June reminded them. "We don't want that for her, do we?"

"No, of course not," Harry agreed. "I think everything will work out just fine. I'm going to go to woodworking and see if I can play around with some of the tools for a while. Wanna' come, too, Zack?"

"Okay! I guess so. I don't have anything better to do," he said, rather unenthusiastically,

"Hey! Don't let me twist your arm," Harry responded.

"Yeah! Sure! That's a good idea! Was that any better?" Zack countered with a slight smile.

"It sure was! Let's go! See you all at dinner," he called over his shoulder as he linked his arm with Zack, and pulled him along towards the woodworking shed.

"I'm going to look for some interesting things to photograph," Carl told the two girls.

"Keep an eye out for good scenery for me to paint, will you?" June asked.

"Sure thing! If it's good to paint, I'm sure it will make a good photo, too," he replied, and disappeared down the path.

"You want to go and sit by the lake and just talk, June?" Shelley shyly asked.

"I think that's a fine idea on a fine day like this," she answered. "Let's go!"

CHAPTER FIVE

Next morning dawned bright and sunny. There were a few fair weather clouds in the sky, looking like fluffy sheep against the sparkling blue. It was a lovely day for a field trip that would be a full day in the fresh air.

"Everybody up and attum," Mr. Hank called out from the doorway of the boys' cabin. "It's seven o'clock, and the days a 'wastin'. Breakfast will be on the table in thirty minutes. I'm going on ahead to get our table. Last one there has to do the cleanup," and the door banged shut behind him.

"He's as annoying a waker upper as my Mom with the broom handle." Carl groaned, and rolled over, nearly ending up on the floor. His bunk in the cabin was half as wide as his bed at home, and he wasn't used to it yet.

Zack hadn't moved at all. Harry sat up, swung his long legs to the floor, and stretched his arms over his head. He yawned, then said, "I don't mind getting up early. In fact, this is later than I have to get up for school at home. Classes at our school start at 7:30, so this is a treat for me," he said to no one in particular.

"So, go be cheery somewhere else," muttered Zack. "It should be against the law to be cheerful before breakfast."

"Okay! Zack. Get the lead out. We don't want to be the last ones there," Carl encouraged him.

"Yeah! Yeah! What's the rush? They'll have plenty. Give me a break. Getting up is always a shock to my system." Zack was really having a hard time getting his eyes open. His pillow fell to the floor as he struggled to untangle himself from the blanket and sit up.

"You need some help there?" Harry teased. "Here, take my hand," and he held it out.

"Aw, just go away. I'm gettin' up! I'm gettin' up!" And he stretched over the covers to reach his pile of clothes which lay across the foot locker at the end of his bed. On the second attempt he finally got both feet in the correct legs of his pants and stood up. His shirt nearly ended up on backwards, but Harry reached over just in time to turn it right side to.

"Are we all ready?" asked Carl, standing across the room and holding the door open.

"Yep, we're right behind you," Harry said, guiding a reluctant Zack in the right direction.

"Okay! Okay! I'm up and almost awake. Lead on, oh, fearless leader," Zack was trying to sound halfway agreeable as he did a sort of stumble walk across the room. "Where are we going?" he asked questioningly.

"Duh! To breakfast, dummy!" Carl said.

"Oh! yeah! I knew there was something." Zack mumbled.

By the time the three boys got to the Dining Hall, Ms. C., Shelley, and June had joined Mr. Hank. They were all sitting together at a table near the entrance where they would be sure to see the boys when they arrived,

"Well, and good morning to you sleepy heads," Ms. C. greeted them.

"We almost started without you guys," Shelley added.

"But, we decided to be polite and wait just a few minutes more, and, sure enough, here you are," June said with a smile. "Let's eat! I'm starving."

Breakfast was quiet time for a while as the hungry group filled their plates, and then their stomachs. Mr. Hank was the first to break the silence. "The bus for our trip today will be here at 9:00 in front of the administration building. Remember, we will be there all day, so bring your sunscreen, and a light sweater or jacket, as it may be cooler later in the day. The Dining Hall folks are packing lunches for all of us and we will have a picnic at the village. Any questions?" he finished, and looked at all the attentive faces.

"When are we going to get Lucy? Don't forget Lucy!" Shelley called out.

"Of course we won't forget Lucy," Ms. C. assured her, and gave her a brief hug. "Mr. Hank and I are going over there right now, and see that she is already. You all want to tag along as well?"

"I sure do," Shelley said.

"Me, too," June added.

"Us guys are coming, too, aren't we?" Carl said, and nodded at Zack and Harry.

"Of course," Harry affirmed.

"Guess so," Zack mumbled.

"Okay! Let's do it!" and Mr. Hank was out the door.

When they arrived at the Infirmary, they were pleasantly surprised to see that Lucy was already up, dressed and sitting on the Infirmary porch in the wheelchair. Nurse Kathy was by her side.

"I was wondering where you guys were. I was afraid you had forgotten me," she called down to them. "I'm so happy to see you!" Her smile was as wide as her face.

"I'm so glad you are able to come with us," Shelley said as she hustled onto the porch to stand beside her. "We're going to have a great day," and she gave Lucy's hand a gentle squeeze.

"We could never forget you, Lucy," Carl exclaimed. "Have you had breakfast?"

"Yep! Someone from the Dining Hall brought me some pancakes, juice and milk. It was delicious, and now I'm ready to get out of here-not that you haven't been just wonderful, Nurse Kathy," she quickly added, "but I'm really ready for some excitement."

"Well, just don't get too ready, Lucy. You still have to be careful of any further injury to ankle or shoulder," she admonished. "You all be sure she doesn't do anything too active, just yet, okay?"

"We won't let her do anything but sit, right kids?" June promised.

"Right!" "We won't!" "Nope!" was heard.

"Okay! I think we are as ready as we will ever be," Ms. C said. "The bus will be here soon, so let's get over to the Admin. Building."

"I'll take care of Lucy," Carl announced, and grabbing a hold of the handles, he began to push Lucy and her wheeled chariot to the ramp at the end of the porch. "I promise I won't go too fast, Lucy," he added, as he slowly guided the chair down to level ground and the rest of the group.

"Thank you, Carl. You are an excellent chauffeur," Lucy laughed and looked up at him. "Do you charge by the hour or by the day?"

"For you, there is no charge at all," he replied with a smile. "It is my pleasure to be at your service."

"Okay! Okay! That's enough of the sweet talk. We gotta go get the bus," Zack reminded them, and began to lead the way.

When they arrived at the administration building they saw that most of the camps' population was there, ready for a fun day at the Village. The bus driver was just positioning the vehicle in front of the building. Mr. Matt, the head administrator for the Retreat, was standing on the porch with a number of the counsellors. He raised his hand for quiet so he could be heard as he gave the final instructions for the day's activities.

"You kids are really going to enjoy this unique historical Village. I'm sure your counsellors have already told you about many of the things you will see and do there. There are signs that will direct you in different ways. Please, observe these signs. Be sure you always have a partner with you-no going off on your own. We will meet at the Village Green for lunch. I'm sure you will have found it by that time." That remark got a chuckle from the kids. "Okay, any questions?" Mr. Matt looked around the crowd. "I don't see any hands, so, let's get onto the bus. No pushing. There's room for everybody."

To the excited kids it seemed like the drive to the Village took an hour, but, in a short half hour they were alighting at the Village gates. There they found colorful brochures which included maps of the Village layout. Ms. C and Mr. Hank gathered the Unit Three kids around them.

"Kids, you are on your own for the rest of the day," Mr. Hank said. "But remember not to go off on your own-for any reason. Always have at least one buddy with you at all times. If there is any problem you will find at least one of us at the general store at all times. Please, look at your maps now and find that location." He paused a moment to give them time to find it. "Okay? You got it?"

"Yep!" And affirmative nods answered him.

"Okay, then," Ms. C said. "Off you go, and have a fine time. We'll see you at lunch."

Carl had already gotten Lucy safely off the bus and into her wheelchair. "Where do you want to go Lucy?" Carl asked. "Your wish is my command."

"I'd really like to see the farm, and maybe get the chance to pat some of the animals," she looked wistfully up at him. "How about you?"

"That sounds great to me. I don't think I have ever patted any animal except my cat, Pinto," he replied.

"Oh, you have a cat?" Lucy's eyes widened in surprise. "You didn't tell me that before. I wish we could have one, but my dad's allergic to them-at least he says he is."

"Well, I'm pretty sure they will have a cat at the farm here. Cats are really handy animals to have around a barn where there are usually mice and rats," Carl told her as he pushed the wheelchair down the path indicating the way to the farm. "See you guys at lunch," he said with a wave at the others.

June turned to Shelley. "What are you interested in, Shelley?"

"I was just reading about the weaving and spinning they do at the farm house," she answered. "There is always someone there demonstrating how cloth was made in the homes. They even let some of the Village visitors give it a try. How does that sound to you?"

"Yeah! I'd really like to see that. I saw someone doing that in an old movie on TV last week. It looked fascinating. Let's go!" And they left Zack and Harry standing at the entrance-each perusing his brochure. They didn't think for a moment that the boys would be interested in such things as spinning and weaving.

"That leaves you and me," Harry spoke the obvious to Zack. "See anything you'd particularly like to see?"

"Yeah! In fact, I actually do. It says they have a print shop here-one that used to put out a weekly newspaper. I'm really interested in mechanical things. I think that's what I'd like to do as a career-when

I finish school, of course," Zack looked a little embarrassed at having said so much. He stood looking shyly at Harry.

"Where's that in this brochure? It sounds like a great idea," Harry answered with enthusiasm. "Which way do we go?"

"It says it's down by the river. I think that is down this path here on the right," Zack indicated the path on his map, then turned and headed where his finger pointed, and Harry fell in step beside him.

By that time Carl and Lucy had arrived at the barn. Sure enough, there was not just one cat, but two, and one had a litter of four kittens. "Oh, they are so cute," Lucy exclaimed. "Do you think I can hold one?"

"Let's ask that man by the barn door. He looks like he works here," Carl advised.

The man had noticed their interest and had started walking over to them. "Those kittens are about four weeks old, and you can pick them up if you'd like," he said. "They like to be petted and the mother cat, that orange tabby cat over there," and he gestured to the barn door, "is the mother. She doesn't mind it at all. Inside the barn we have some other baby animals, calves, puppies, lambs, and there are some piglets in the sty behind the barn. Even the goats have some kids out in the field."

"Wow! Can we touch all of them?" Lucy was thrilled at the thought of so many small animals.

"Well, you can try, but some of them are shy and others aren't within reach of the fencing," Bob (the name on the man's badge) said. "And some of the mother's don't want their babies handled, so they won't come close enough. The wheel chair might scare them, but you can give it a try."

Lucy looked imploringly at Carl. "Let's try, okay? We'll be very careful, and as quiet as we can," she promised.

"Sure thing," Carl agreed. "Let's do it!" And they spent the next hour or more in the barn and yard at the farm. After petting and playing with the kittens, they approached a black and white cow, and had the chance to pat her calf and feed it from a bottle. The mother sheep came over to the fence to nuzzle them for food and her lamb came with her. Lucy was delighted with the feel of its fur-it was the softest thing she had ever touched. They were both astonished to see how many babies the mother pig had. There must have been at least eleven of them. The baby goats were a lot of fun to watch. They were running, jumping, and butting each other, and the big goats as well, falling over each other as they climbed the rocks, and even over the bushes and shrubs around the field. Carl and Lucy couldn't stop laughing at their antics.

Meanwhile, Shelley and June were in the farmhouse, watching some very skilled ladies spinning and weaving. They went over to watch a woman dressed in the costume of an earlier generation. She was very carefully separating fine fibers and feeding them onto a fine thread that was connected to even longer threads leading to the spinning wheel. "Excuse me, please. Can you tell us how the spinning wheel works?" June asked Alice (according to the badge she wore).

Alice smiled and set her work aside. "It looks like magic, doesn't it?" she said. "But it is quite simple once you understand the process." She reached into a bag at her feet and pulled put a clump of grayish fur. "It starts with wool which looks like this and comes from the sheep we have here at the village. The sheep are shorn in the spring. That's when they are shaved of all the fur that has kept them nice and toasty warm all winter."

"Don't they get scared when that happens to them?" Shelley asked.

"Well, maybe the first time it happens," Alice explained. "But it is actually a big help to the sheep who then don't have to wear a wooly fur coat all summer in the heat."

"Oh, of course they would feel better then," Shelley nodded. "Then what happens to the wool?"

"After all the sheep are shorn, the wool is thoroughly washed-sheep aren't good at taking baths, you know, so the wool is pretty dirty." June and Shelley laughed at that. "Now the wool is called 'fleece' and it moves to the next step towards becoming cloth, which is 'carding'." Alice picked up two paddles which looked like large hairbrushes. There were short, thin metal spikes on them like hairbrush bristles-only sharper.

"I'm glad my hairbrush has plastic bristles," June commented. "Those bristles look pretty sharp."

"Well, they have a big job to do for the next step in our process," and Alice went on with her lesson. "Now I will take a small portion of the fleece and stick it on the bristles of one of the paddles, like so," and she demonstrated. "Then I will take the other paddle and comb the fleece onto it. This begins to straighten the fleece and pull any snags out of it. See?" and she held up the paddle.

"That would hurt the sheep if he was still wearing his coat, I think." Shelley said. "I hate it when my hair gets snags in it."

"You have a good point there," Alice agreed. "I continue using these paddles in this way until all the fleece is nice and straight and free of any debris. Then it is ready for the spinning wheel." She turned her chair around to the large wheel that was standing on the floor behind her. A big basket of clean, soft wool was beside the wheel. Alice took a small clump of the wool and gently pulled a few strands away from the larger clump, but still remained attached to it.

"Now I'm going to attach this small strand to that already on my wheel and begin to rotate the wheel with this foot pedal. I will continue to gently feed the strands of wool to the wheel which is going to put a twist to the strands to make the thread that you can see beginning to wind around this bobbin," and Alice pointed to the bobbin to her left on the end of the spinning wheel while she began to set the wheel spinning. June and Shelley were spellbound as they watched thin thread start to pile up on the bobbin.

"Wow! It does seem like magic," Shelley enthused.

"Watching that wheel go round and around would put me in a trance if I looked at it too long," June said. "But if I had lived in those days I would ask to do all the spinning. It seems like a very relaxing chore."

Alice stilled the wheel and smiled at both the girls. "Yes, it is relaxing, but imagine <u>having</u> to sit here for hours and hours, just spinning and spinning because the thread was needed for the weaver to make the cloth-to make the clothes for all the family. That's a pretty big responsibility."

"Yeah, I guess it would get pretty old, pretty fast when you put it that way," June agreed. "Thank you for taking the time to show-and tell-us all about making thread."

"Yes. It was a wonderful demonstration. Is anyone going to be weaving again today? No one seems to be there right now," Shelley asked, and pointed over to the loom on the other side of the room, which was no longer in operation.

"There will be a weaving demonstration again at 1:00 this afternoon," Alice answered. "If you come back then you will be able to see how that is done. Come a little bit earlier so you will be able to get a front row seat," she advised.

"We will," Shelley promised. "And thank you again for your super presentation. I hope we will see you later," she added as she and June left through the farmhouse kitchen where a baking demonstration had just finished, and the room was full of delicious aromas.

"Where to next?" June asked.

"I'd just like to walk around and see what's happening in different places. Is that okay with you?" Shelley asked.

"Sounds like a fine idea. That way we can be surprised and delighted with whatever we see," June replied. "Let's go! Maybe we will bump into some of the others."

They would have 'bumped' into Harry and Zack if they had turned left at the village green. As it was, they turned right instead and didn't meet up with them until lunch. Harry and Zack had, at first, headed for the print shop, by way of the river bank. It wasn't long, though, before Harry saw a sign for the blacksmith shop. Suddenly memory kicked in and Harry remembered a poem he had read in freshman English class, 'The Village Blacksmith'. It had stayed in his head because of the thoughtful description of a blacksmith's life the poet had written. He couldn't remember the poet's name, but the poem had stuck with him.

"Hey, Zack! What about the blacksmith? I think they were some of the early mechanics-you know, working with iron and other metals? It looks like it is on the way to the print shop," Harry suggested.

"Well, I guess so, cause it's on the way. But I don't want to stay long," Zack grudgingly responded.

"No, we won't, especially if there isn't any demonstration," Harry agreed.

There was a small crowd at the entrance to the blacksmith shop. Harry worked his way closer to the front with Zack right behind. "Excuse me! Excuse me!" he kept apologizing. He knew he was being rude, but he really wanted to see a blacksmith, and his 'large and sinewy hands', for himself. And he wasn't disappointed. The man standing at the front of the crowd was indeed a large man with very muscular shoulders and arms. But his face had a kind and gentle look. He held a very impressive hammer in his right hand.

"Welcome to my forge-the proper name for a blacksmiths shop," the kind man said as he looked at all the people who had come to see his work. "I am Tom and I am a blacksmith. Almost anything in the village made of iron needs my help. A blacksmith must especially be an expert in horseshoeing. And he needs to be strong. Most of his customers weigh a lot more than he does," (some people in the audience laughed at this comment) "and he has to be able to control them for this very important-and dangerous-task. I have a very important job. And one of the most important jobs I have is keeping the village horses in tip-top shape-which mainly means caring for their feet." Tom paused to take a deep breath and wipe the sweat from his brow. Then he raised his left hand in which he held a set of iron pincers, which in turn held a glowing horse shoe. "Here in my hand you see a horseshoe. The horse shoe needs to fit a particular horse's hoof. Just like you all have different size feet, so do horses. They can't wear just anyone's shoes," he was explaining. "In the early days of our American country horses were as important as your cars are today. They were the fastest way to get anywhere-if need be, and their feet were especially important." The blacksmith laid the horseshoe down on a large block of iron. "This is my anvil. This is where I shape and form the right horseshoe for the correct horse's hoof. You can see my fire here behind me, and my pail of cold water here at my feet. Next to my fire you can see that large pile of canvas colored material with the long set of handles at one end." He pointed at the thing he had just described. "Those are 'bellows'. Does anyone know what bellows are for?"

Much to Zack's surprise, Harry raised his hand.

"Yes, young man?" and the blacksmith nodded at Harry.

"I think they are used to pump air on the fire to keep it hot enough to get the iron ready for shaping," Harry answered.

"You are absolutely correct! What's your name, young man?" he asked.

Now Harry was a little embarrassed at being the center of attention. "Um, uh, Harry, Harry Milton."

"Well done, Harry Milton! Would you like to give me a hand with this part of the demonstration?" Tom asked.

"Um, um, okay! What do you want me to do?" Harry stammered.

"I'd like you to use the bellows on the fire while I hold my horseshoe in the coals to get it red hot again. It has cooled off while I have been talking. Can you do that?" Tom queried.

"I can do that, sure," Harry readily answered. Now he was a little hyped about actually getting involved. "Where do I stand?"

"Right over there behind the bellows," Tom directed. "Now, get a good grip on the handles. You're just going to open and close the bellow's handles as strongly as you can. The fire needs to be over 2500 degrees to do its job. That's a whole lot of air. Let's get to it. Are you ready, Harry?"

"Ready as I'll ever be," he responded, as he took a good hold on the bellow's handles and pushed them together as hard as he could. A blast of air whooshed into the fire and ashes rose to the roof. The coals began to glow brightly, and Tom lowered the tongs holding the horse shoe into the heart of the flaming embers. After a minute or two, the horse shoe also began to glow. Tom turned it over and rested the other side in the embers. Then he removed it, placed it on the anvil and banged it hard in a few places. Then he dunked it into the pail of water. The hiss of heated metal meeting cold water could be heard by all in the attentive audience.

Tom held the dripping horseshoe up for all to see. "If I had a horse here, I would now measure this shoe to its hoof and check for size. I would continue this process until the shoe and the hoof matched perfectly, and then I would use these special nails," he paused and reached into a wooden box sitting on his bench. He withdrew two small nails which he held aloft for all the see, "and nail the shoe to its hoof. And 'No' it doesn't hurt the horse because his hoof is made of the same material as our own fingernails." At this point Tom stopped talking and looked around at his visitor. "Now, are there any questions?" he continued. No one raised a hand, and many people began to move off towards other village exhibits.

"Let's give a big hand to Harry for his help!" Tom encouraged. "Thank you, Harry! You did a fine job," he complemented him as he shook his hand warmly.

"It was really fun for me. Thank you for giving me the chance to participate," Harry responded with a grin. "I truly enjoyed it."

Zack had been standing off to the side, impatiently waiting for Harry to rejoin him so they could continue to the print shop. "Get the lead out, Harry. The day's running on. Com'on, let's go!"

"Thanks again for letting me help, Tom," Harry said, and with a brief salute, he turned and hurried after Zack.

"Jeez! I thought you were getting ready to marry the guy, Harry," Zack said petulantly as Harry caught up to him.

"Zack, take it easy. I didn't want to be rude to Tom. We have a lot more of the day. Let's enjoy it, okay?" And Harry rested his arm on Zack's shoulder as they ambled on to find the print shop.

The morning passed quickly for all the kids. Soon it was lunch time.

Lucy couldn't stop talking about all the animals she and Carl had seen and patted. "I think the lambs were the sweetest babies ever. With their soft, wooly fur and cute little faces-they were so adorable," she rhapsodized to anyone who would listen.

"She was trying to figure out how she could convince her parents to start a farm," Carl added. "I don't think that will go over very well, though. They live in a third floor apartment." Everyone laughed at that.

"Well, maybe I can have my own farm when I get out of school," Lucy optimistically pointed out.

"One can always dream," June agreed.

"We learned how cloth gets made, and that is probably a more practical dream than starting a farm," Shelley suggested.

"What, you want to become a dressmaker?" Harry asked.

"No, silly! I just meant working with cloth is a lot easier than working with a farm and animals," Shelley answered.

"I've decided I'm gonna' become a newspaper man instead of a machinist," Zack announced. "Man, watching that old press, and hearing the guy talk about the early days of newspapers-that was really interesting, and exciting, didn't you think, Harry?"

"Yeah, it was. If I had lived in those times I would have had a difficult time deciding between blacksmithing and reporting," Harry answered, "But setting all those tiny type letters sure would be a challenge-especially as you had to set them backwards," he added.

"It sure sounds like you all had great adventures this morning," Ms. C said.

"And you still have the afternoon for more," Mr. Hank cheerfully assured them. "Let's finish lunch so we can go off and find them. We certainly will have a lot to talk about around the campfire back at the Retreat tonight."

The afternoon passed as quickly as the morning had, as all the campers continued to explore the village, and find things of interest. Some things were completely new to them such as churning butter, and collecting honey. Others, they were a little more familiar with, like wood working and quilting. All in all it was a very fine day, and a very fine outing. Campers and counsellors alike were ready to head back to the Retreat in the late afternoon, looking forward to a hearty supper, and some campfire time before bed.

CHAPTER SIX

The next morning the sun rose into a brilliantly clear blue sky. Ms. C. went about shaking the feet of Lucy, Shelley, and June. "Time to get up girls. It's a beautiful morning, telling us we are going to have a fine day. And we don't want to waste a moment of it."

"It can't be morning," Lucy said around a yawn. "I just went to sleep." And she snuggled deeper under the covers.

"No, no, it can't be time to get up. I was in the middle of a beautiful dream," and Shelley turned over to settle back into sleep.

June sat up and stretched towards the ceiling. "Good morning, good morning world. I had a wonderful night's sleep!" She swung her legs to the floor and stood up. "What's on our agenda for today, Ms. C?"

"There are no particular activities on our schedule for this morning," she answered. "Mr. Hank and I have some paper work to do, so you are on your own to choose for yourselves," she told them. "I think you started learning to swim the other day, didn't you Shelley?"

"Yes, that's right. I was getting the hang of it pretty good, too" she answered, and rolled over. "I think I'll go to the lake and get another lesson. But first, I'm hungry. I'll beat you all to the Dining Hall," she added as she tumbled out of bed.

"Hey, no fair. I have to wait for my chauffeur," Lucy wailed.

The nurse had checked Lucy out when the group returned to the Retreat the evening before, and deemed her well enough to go back to the cabin with the others. However, she restricted her to the use of the wheelchair for one more day-just to be on the safe side. Lucy had complained, but Nurse Kathy stood firm-it was the chair for one more day, or the infirmary for the night. Lucy really wanted to get back to her cabin and friends. Nurse Kathy won that one, and Carl had no objection to being Lucy's devoted slave-as needed-for one more day.

"That's okay, Lucy," June said. "I'll be your substitute driver if Carl sleeps in. And I'm sure there will be plenty of food whenever we get there. Do you need any help getting dressed?" she offered.

"Oh, Lucy, I didn't mean anything by it. I'm sorry. I just wasn't thinking straight yet. Of course we'll all go together," Shelley apologized.

"That's okay, Shelley! I know you didn't mean anything bad by it. I often put my foot in my mouth, too," Lucy responded with a smile. "I'm okay getting dressed if someone can just hand me my shirt and jeans from the hook."

"Here! Catch!" June called out, and sailed the clothes across the bunks.

Lucy reached up and caught them just as they were about to wrap around her head. "Thanks, June. I'll be quick!"

"I'll meet you all in the Dining Hall," Ms. C. said as she headed out the door. "Don't dilly-dally!"

In no time at all the three girls were ready to go. June got Lucy's wheelchair outside and safely placed for Lucy's ascent down the cabin stairs. Leaning on Shelley, Lucy easily hop-hopped down the steps and plunked herself in the seat. Just as they started down the wooded path they heard the boys noisily headed their way.

"I'm coming! I'm coming," Carl's voice rang out over the others.

"We're all coming!" Harry yelled.

"Yeah, yeah!" grumbled Zack as the boys appeared.

"I'll take over, June," Carl offered.

"Be my guest, young sir," June said and stepped back from the wheelchair.

"Next stop, the Dining Hall," Carl announced. What are you going to do after breakfast, Lucy?" he asked.

"Oh, dear! I haven't really thought about that yet. Shelley, you're going to the lake, right?" she queried.

"Yep! That's my plan!" she affirmed.

"That's right. You didn't have a chance to choose an activity at the Infirmary, did you?" June asked.

"Nope! And I'm open to suggestions now," Lucy replied.

"I chose Arts and Crafts, and I've started a painting-watercolors. I'm looking forward to getting back to work on it," June said.

"I've gotten interested in photography," Carl volunteered, "but that wouldn't be so great for you-at least not for today," he added.

"And we've gotten into wood working, me and Zack," Harry told her. "I guess that wouldn't be such a good idea for you, either, I don't think, huh?" And he looked questioningly at her.

"Girls don't do wood working, dodo," Zack said disgustedly.

"Well, I could try it if I wanted to, smarty pants," Lucy defended Harry. "It just so happens that I'm not interested in it. June, can I go to Arts and Crafts with you this morning? I'm sure I will find something of interest there."

"Of course you can. I'll be happy to have you with me. It will be fun!"

"But first, to the Dining Hall!" Shelley reminded them all.

After a hearty breakfast the kids all went their separate ways, all except Carl who first delivered Lucy, along with June, to the Arts and Crafts building. From there he headed over to the photography studio to collect a camera, lenses and other things he might need, or want, while exploring for just the right photos. And so the morning passed, until the dinner gong sounded and lunch was ready. From all corners of the Retreat kids came flocking for the noonday meal.

Shelley was the first of Unit Three to arrive, her hair not yet dry from her swimming lesson. Soon Harry and Zack appeared out of the woods next to the sports field. Harry waved to Shelley. "Look what I made," he shouted, and held up a square-looking object.

"What is it?" she called back. "I can't see it very well from here."

"You'd think he invented a cure for cancer with all his excitement over a simple little picture frame," Zack commented as they drew closer.

"Now, Zack," Shelley scowled at him. "It may seem 'simple' to you, but Harry did it by himself and has every reason to be proud of what he created," she continued as she admired the results of Harry's efforts. "What did you make? Let me see!" and she held out her hand.

"No, it ain't nothing," and Zack kept his hand behind his back.

"Zack made one, too," Harry said. "I think his is really fine-better than mine because he did some fancy whittling on the wood before he put it together. Com'on Zack, show Shelley!" he urged.

Zack looked embarrassed. "Nah! It ain't nothing!"

"But I really want to see it," Shelley encouraged. "Please?"

"Aw right, but don't laugh, okay," he implored, his face getting redder by the minute. By this time June and Lucy had arrived, June huffing a little as she maneuvered Lucy's wheelchair across the rocky driveway in front of the Dining Hall.

"What're you guys doing?" Lucy asked. "Have you been waiting for us?"

"Sort of, but, not really," Shelley answered. "I got here just a few minutes before Harry and Zack-not two minutes ago. They were just showing me the picture frames they made in wood working. Show them you guys!"

"Yeah, we want to see," Lucy implored.

"And I want to show off my painting," June said. "After you, of course, Zack!"

Zack, in a bit of a defiant way, stuck his picture frame out in front of him, half expecting a burst of unkind laughter to greet his work.

"Oh! Wow!" June said, praise evident in her tone.

"That is really beautiful," Shelley breathed out.

"See, I told you so!" Harry smacked Zack gently in the back.

A new voice joined the chatter. "Are you guys all standing out here waiting for me?" Carl called out. "I had to take the photography equipment back to the photo shop first. That's what took me so long. "How very thoughtful of you to wait, but you really shouldn't have!" he added.

"And we didn't!" was Zack's comment.

"We are all having a 'show 'n' tell," Shelley told him. "Harry and Zack have made really great picture frames in wood working shop. We're trying to decide whose is the best. Show him!" she directed the two boys.

"He can see them just fine, Shelley! What's the big deal?" Zack had had just about enough of this impromptu art show.

"Hey! What are you kids waiting for? Lunch is being served-NOW!" Mr. Hank was standing on the porch of the Dining Hall, gesturing for the kids to get up there.

"Okay! Okay! We're coming!" Harry assured him with a wave. "Let's go before they close the doors on us," he advised the group with a grin. "You can all see our frames later."

"And my painting, too," June reminded them.

"And your painting, too!" Harry agreed.

So, with Carl now in charge of the wheelchair, they all went in to a fine and satisfying lunch, picture frames and paintings forgotten for the moment.

"This afternoon we are going to play kick ball with Unit Four," Mr. Hank announced just as lunch was winding down. "I've arranged it with Mr. Shaker and Ms. Alton. They have eight kids, but that's not a problem in kick ball. You guys will just have more turns being 'up'. Okay?"

"That's no problem for us, Mr. Hank. We'll run right over them," Zack assured him. "Won't we, team?" and he looked around at his fellow Unit members.

"If you say so, Zack," Harry agreed with a smile.

"Lucy, you can keep score, okay?" Mr. Hank asked.

"Sure! I'm good at that," she agreed.

The teams were fairly evenly matched in terms of ability, but Unit Three had to work a little harder, with their handicap of fewer numbers. However, at the end of the game Unit Five had only beaten them by two points 23-21- not a bad showing- not bad at all Mr. Hank assured them as they left the sport field, tired but contented.

"It's private time until dinner," Ms. C. announced as they neared their area. "But Lucy, the nurse wants to check you over once more before she takes you off the disabled list. If you check out fine, you will be free of that wheelchair. How does that sound?"

"Great! Should I go now?" she asked.

"Yes, she is expecting you. I'll go with you to get the official report. Carl, can you wheel her over?" Ms. C. looked at him.

"Sure! I'll be glad to," he readily agreed.

It was a short walk to the Infirmary where Nurse Kathy was, indeed, waiting to see Lucy. "How are you doing, Lucy?" she greeted them, with a nod and a smile for Carl and Ms. C.

"I'm feeling very well, Nurse Kathy, and I am definitely ready to return this wheelchair," she announced brightly, and bounced up from her seat.

"Don't get too spunky, too quickly, Missy. Let me check you over and I'll be the judge of just how you're doing," Nurse Kathy advised her.

"Okay! I'm just excited," Lucy apologized. "I don't want to feel like an invalid anymore."

"I know you don't, she said. "So let's get that checkup over with. "Ms. C., you and Carl can wait out on the porch. We won't be very long, I don't think."

"Okay! See you in a bit, Lucy," Ms. C. said, and she led the way out the door.

"Do you think Lucy will get the all clear, Ms. C.?" Carl asked with a worried frown crinkling his forehead.

"I'm pretty sure she will, Carl. You have been a wonderful chauffeur for her," she complimented him, "and she has been a good patient. I think she will get a very good report. Not to worry!"

"I sure hope so," Carl said, and he sat down on the porch steps to wait.

They didn't have to wait too long. "I'm all better," announced a very happy Lucy, seeming to dance out of the Infirmary.

"Now, wait just one minute, young lady," Nurse Kathy interrupted from the doorway. "I just gave you some instructions, didn't I?"

"Yes, Nurse Kathy, you did! I just got carried away with my freedom. You told me: No running, no jumping, no skipping, no dancing for another day or two. And I promised I won't, didn't I?"

"Yes, you did, but I'm not sure I can trust you to keep your promise. I needed to hear it said to your friends as well. I think I can sign you off the disabled list now." Nurse Kathy gave Lucy a big smile and a gentle hug. Then she turned to Ms. C. and handed her some papers. "Here is the 'official' report. I'll call Lucy's parents and tell them the good news. You all have a good afternoon," she said, and returned to her office.

"Well, that is surely good news," Ms. C. said. She, also, had a big smile for the kids. "You have the rest of the afternoon for private time. Remember to take it slow Lucy. I'll see you both at dinner! Have fun!" and she left them standing there.

"I'm so glad you're doing good, Lucy. Did you have any plans for this afternoon?" Carl shyly asked.

"Um, no I didn't make any plans 'cause I didn't know what the nurse was going to say, and if I would still be tied to that old wheelchair," she said.

"Well, I have been wanting to take a canoe out on the lake, and you should really have two people to do that. Besides, that is the rule for all us kids here-no one can go out in a canoe alone," he finished explaining in a rush. "What do you think?"

"I'm thinking that would be a lot of fun. Do you think we could really do it?" she asked questioningly.

"Well, we won't know if we don't try, and we don't have to go very far this first time out. I know the life guard at the waterfront will give us good instructions before we even get in the canoe, and, of course, we will have to wear life jackets. Let's try!" he encouraged.

"Okay! You've talked me into it," Lucy replied excitedly.

At the waterfront they found Peter, the lifeguard, and introduced themselves.

"Happy to meet you, kids. Do either of you have any experience with canoes?" he asked.

"Nope!" Carl said and shook his head.

"No, but I read a story about some mountain men and they went all over the rivers in canoes," Lucy offered.

"Well, we aren't going anywhere near that far today," Peter replied with a smile. "First, we are going to fit you both with life jackets, and then we are going to check out the canoes that are tied along the shore, over there, away from the swimming area," and he led the way to where the life jacket were hanging in the sun. "Look them over carefully, and find ones that fit you snugly-but are not too tight."

The looking over didn't take long. "I like this one," and Lucy held up a bright red one. "It seems to fit me," she added as she fastened the straps.

"This yellow one looks good for me," Carl said.

"Okay kids, let me just give a light yank on each of you to make sure they are snug enough," Peter explained. "Good job! Now for the canoe to go with them." It was a short walk along the shore to where the canoes were lined up, half in the water and half on the shore.

"Before we even move one of these crafts, there are a few very important things to know about a canoe, especially compared to a row boat, for example." Peter paused and looked at them seriously. "Canoes are very tippy, and you should never stand up in one. If you did, you would be flipped into the water faster than you could say 'Mighty Mouse!'"

The kids laughed at that.

"Yeah, that's a funny saying, but it wouldn't be funny if it happened, because getting back into a canoe in deep water is very hard, for even the best of canoers," he explained further. "But we won't worry about that for today because you aren't going to stand up, right?" Peter said firmly and gave them a stern look.

"No! No! Of course we won't," Carl assured him, and Lucy nodded her head vigorously. "Okay, which one do you like, Lucy? Take your pick."

"Well, they all sorta look alike, don't you think, Carl?" she asked him.

"You got a point there, Lucy, but do you have a favorite color?" he was being very much a gentleman.

"Blue is my favorite color, but light blue, and the blue canoe here is really dark. Maybe the orange one?" she suggested.

"Yeah! I like orange, and you can see it really well on the water," he agreed. And so the orange one it was.

Peter lifted the end that rested on the shore and guided it between the others, until it was fully in the shallow water. Carl and Lucy followed behind.

"Okay, kids. Now remember what I said about canoes being very tippy," he reminded them. "They won't seem tippy here at the shore as the lake bottom is only inches away, but don't let that fool you. Lucy, why don't you get in the front, and Carl, here at the back." The kids climbed into their places.

"All comfy?" he asked.

"Not quite like my easy chair at home, but not bad for a boat," Lucy responded.

"Canoe," Carl reminded her. "You don't want to insult her, do you?" he joked. "And I think water craft are always referred to as 'she', aren't they, Peter?" he added.

"You're right," Peter affirmed. "I know there's a particular reason, but I can't remember what it is."

"Oh, no! I definitely wouldn't want to insult her," Lucy exclaimed and settled on her bench seat

"Okay, then. Paddling! These are paddles, not oars," and Peter held up a pair of short paddles. To go straight, one of you paddles on the right hand side of the canoe and the other on the left. Try to match the strength of your strokes to each other. It is the job of the one in the back to gauge the way the front person is stroking and try to match it for power." Peter paused in his instruction. "Carl, that's you now. And go easy! A canoe is a very gentle type of water craft-a little power goes a long way. Paddling on the left only will turn the canoe to the right, and the opposite is true for paddling on the right. So…"Peter was interrupted by a shriek from Lucy

"Opps! I almost forgot." Lucy turned around to look at Carl and Peter, seeming close to tears, a look of embarrassment on her face. "I have to be easy on my shoulder as well as my ankle, for a few more days," Lucy voice quavered as she spoke. "But I really want to try this," she quickly added.

"Oh! I'm so sorry, Lucy! I'm such a dunce! What was I thinking? Obviously, I wasn't. We can't do this!" Carl was overcome with guilt.

"Now, just hold on for a moment," Peter interjected. "Here you are, all set for a canoe ride. It is very possible for one person to handle a canoe just fine. Remember those mountain men, Lucy? They handled their canoes all by themselves. Carl, are you still ready to give this a try?"

"Well, yeah, but what about Lucy?" He looked confused.

"Lucy, are you comfortable sitting there? Would you like to keep Carl company while he learns how to guide a canoe?" Peter asked.

"Oh, boy! Would I!" Hope was evident in her voice. "It will still be great fun, Carl. I trust you. I'll pretend I'm Cleopatra going down the Nile," was her enthusiastic reply, and she swiped at some tears that had begun to run down her cheek.

"Well, if you're sure, Lucy. We won't go very far-maybe just along the shore. That way, if we have any trouble, we can wade to land. How does that sound?" Carl said hopefully.

"Wonderful! What are we waiting for?" A happy smiled returned to her face.

"Okay, then! Oh, one more thing. If you want to slow down or even stop, drag your paddle in the water, flat side to the direction you are headed, and hold it there. Now, have fun, and I'll meet you back here in a half hour or so," Peter said as he gently pushed the canoe a little further into the lake.

Carl gave a couple gentle paddles on the left. Sure enough the canoe veered towards the shore on their right.

"Oops, we don't want to get beached so soon," and he switched his paddle to the right side. With a few more strokes they were gliding silently along the shore. Carl got the hang of paddling first on one side, and then the other, to keep the canoe moving forward.

"This is lovely, Carl," Lucy said, dangling her hand in the water. "It's really peaceful." Just then a deep roaring sound rolled over the lake. It seemed to come from just around the bend they were approaching. "What was that?" Startled, Lucy sat up straight, rocking the canoe.

"I don't know." Carl stopped paddling. "It sounded like an animal. I heard something similar on an animal show I saw last month, but I don't remember what kind of animal it was."

The kids continued watching the shore as the canoe maintained its slow glide across the water, headed a little further towards the center of the lake. Carl adjusted the direction with a gentle paddle on the left, keeping the canoe closer to the shore as it rounded the bend.

"Carl," Lucy whispered. "Look! There, beside that huge rock at the shore. There is a big, dark brown animal getting a drink from the lake."

"Where? Oh! I see it now." At that moment, the animal stood up and gazed across the water. "Oh! Wow! It's a bear!" Carl spoke in a hushed voice, and stilled his paddle, adding drag to its forward motion, slowing them even more.

The two kids sat very still, pretty much holding their breath as they watched the magnificent animal survey its surroundings. Its nose was raised in the air, testing the scents around. It seemed to be contented with what the breeze had to say, and turned with ease to disappear into the woods behind it.

"Oh, my goodness!" Lucy breathed out, in a whisper.

"I wish I had my camera," Carl said. "That was fantastic! The other kids aren't going to believe us."

"Yes, they will," Lucy assured him. "When we tell them, they will be so envious. I can hardly wait for dinner time when we will all be together. Can you turn us around in this canoe?"

"Yeah! I think I have the knack of it now." The canoe easily responded to Carl's maneuvering, and soon they were headed back the way they had come. Peter was at the water's edge when they came in sight of the camp waterfront, and greeted them with a big wave.

"Well, how was it?" he asked before the canoe had even bumped the shore.

"We saw a huge bear," Lucy burst out, unable to contain her excitement.

"Yes, it was super!" Carl added, as he climbed out of the craft, and turned to help Lucy out as well.

"Great! That's not really surprising as there are a number of bear in these woods," Peter said. "But you were very lucky to sight one as we don't get to see them very often. Where was it?"

"Well, we went along the shore and around the bend where the forest juts out into the lake, and there it was, getting a drink from the lake. We didn't seem to scare it, and maybe it didn't even see us," Carl was still trying to get over the wonderful surprise himself. How often does anyone get to see a for real bear? He was still in awe.

"Yeah!" Lucy said. "It finished drinking, took a sniff of the air, and then went back into the woods. It was beautiful," she sighed. "I don't think I'll ever forget that sight."

"Well, you got a special treat," Peter told them. "The other kids will be hoping to see one too, I think."

"Thanks for the canoe lesson," Carl said. "We may come down for another try before we leave," he added.

"I'll be glad to see you any time," Peter assured them. "It's nearly dinner time so you kids better head over to the Dining Hall. I'm getting hungry, too!"

"Okay! See you over there," Lucy smiled her thanks.

CHAPTER SEVEN

The Dining Hall was filling up fast by the time Carl and Lucy got there. June and Shelley could be seen coming up the path from the Arts and Crafts building. Harry and Zack were already on the porch of the Dining Hall, hanging out with a group of boys from the other Units. Ms. C and Mr. Hank weren't there yet.

"I'm going to wait for June and Shelley to get here," Lucy told Carl.

"Yeah, I see the guys on the porch," he said. "And I'm really glad you went with me this afternoon. It was awesome!"

"Me, too! See you inside! Hey June, Shelley!" Lucy called out, and went to meet them. "You'll never guess-Carl and I went out in a canoe, and….."

Carl watched her meet up with the other girls, then went over to stand with the other boys waiting for the Dining Hall doors to open for dinner.

Ms. C. and Mr. Hank arrived just as they did, and Unit Three members met up at their usual table, full of news of their latest adventures.

"If I remember correctly," Ms. C. spoke over the noise of everyone getting settled down at their tables, "there are some handicrafts for us all the see. Are those still available to us?" she inquired.

"After lunch, I took our picture frames to the cabin to keep them safe while we played kickball," Harry said,

"Yeah, he took mine, too," Zack concurred, glad of a reprieve from show 'n' tell again.

"My painting is also at our cabin-for the same reason," June said. "Can we have a campfire after dinner, Ms. C., and we could show our artwork then?"

"That's a great idea, June," Ms. C. said.

"Yes, it is. We were going to suggest that," Mr. Hank added. "It's a beautiful night, just right for a campfire. We can all collect some firewood on our way back to the Unit after dinner."

"It will be the perfect ending for a pretty perfect day," Lucy sighed and looked happily around the table.

"Yes, I think so, too," Shelley agreed.

"Let's eat! All this chatter is making me very hungry," Zack interrupted.

"Okay! Chow down kids!" Mr. Hank matched his words to his actions and took a big mouthful of mashed potatoes.

Before long plates were empty and the kids were full. There was a mad scramble to the door. Many Units had planned campfires for the evening, and there was a scramble to collect the firewood that was available.

"Campfire, here we come," Lucy sang out exuberantly.

"Don't get too excited, Lucy" Ms. C reminded her. "Take care with that ankle!" As they left the Dining Hall, headed to their cabins for light jackets against the evening's chill, they were also eagerly searching the woods for fallen limbs and twigs of all sizes. Before long, they had collected enough fuel to give them an hour or two of a cozy fire under a starlit sky. June, Harry, and Zack had also picked up their art work.

Once everyone was settled around the campfire, Mr. Hank asked, "Is everyone comfortable?" The kids were seated on the fallen logs and large boulders that made up the campfire circle. There were nods and 'yeses' all around. "Wonderful! Now, there is a special activity we like to do around a campfire here at the Retreat. First, we would like you to take some time to think about two activities you do-one that you think you do very well, and one that you don't do so very well and would like to get better at. So, get thinking. When you have your two things in mind, raise your hand to let us know you are ready."

Harry was the first one to raise his hand. Over the next three or four minutes all hands had been raised.

"Okay! Who wants to go first?" Mr. Hank broke the silence. Lucy's hand shot up. "Oh, good. Thank you for being brave, Lucy. You have the stage."

"I'm not all that brave, but you guys make me feel so comfortable with all the special care you have given me, I can't possibly be too nervous with you. Do you want to hear the good thing first-or the not so good one?" she asked.

"There isn't a good or bad to this, Lucy," Ms. C. assured her and smiled encouragingly. "So, whatever feels right for you!"

"Alright then, something I'm good at is playing the piano. My mom started me on lessons when I was five years old. She told me that I started reacting to piano music when I pretty much just a baby. I would smile and squirm around, and bounce up and down, so she decided she would see how I could do with a piano. And I did take to it from the beginning. I have been in a lot of recitals and I often get the highest award." She stopped talking and looked around at all the faces looking back at her.

"Wow! That's great, Lucy. Maybe someday you will play at Carnegie Hall," Carl enthused.

"My Mom thought I would like to play the piano, too, but I didn't like it at all," Shelley said. "I wish I could do that, but…."

"You don't have to be good at everything, Shelley," June sympathized.

"So, what aren't you so good at?" Zack asked abruptly.

"Baking! I can cook like for dinner, vegetables, pasta. Those thing are okay. But when it comes to cakes, or cookies, or any kind of dessert-except maybe Jell-O, I'm a complete failure. My gramma tries to teach me. She says it's easy. But I just can't seem to put something in the oven and have it come out looking like something anyone wants to eat." Lucy heaved a big sigh. "I'm a flop."

"Not to worry, Lucy, there are tons of fast food places all around," Harry consoled her.

"Maybe you'll marry a famous chef, and he can do the cooking while you make a million on the stage," Shelley suggested.

"Things seem to work out as they should," Ms. C. offered. "I don't think you have to worry too much about your meals just now."

"And that's a relief!" were Lucy's last words on the subject.

"Okay," Mr. Hank said. "Who's next?"

"That could be me," Carl raised his hand, and started right in. "I think I am a good runner. I'm on a soccer team at school and I can run that field faster than most of my team mates, and I don't feel all tuckered out at the end of a practice or game. That doesn't mean I'm good at making score. But I can get the ball in the right direction and hand it off to a teammate who has better aim than I do. And I really like doing that."

"Maybe we can challenge another Unit to a soccer match some afternoon," Harry suggested, and looked at Mr. Hank for confirmation.

"Sounds like we could put that into a plan," he agreed.

"I tried out for soccer at my school, but didn't make the team," Zack said. "It's kind of a sissy game anyhow."

"Oh, don't be a sour grape, Zack," June admonished.

"And now, what aren't you so good at?" Ms. C. prompted.

"That's easy! I'm a dunce at history. All those names and dates get all jumbled up. I love historical stories, but putting things in historical order seems impossible and I barely pass my history classes," and Carl sat down.

"What do you want to do as a career? Carl," Mr. Hank asked.

"I haven't really settled on that yet. I'm thinking something with electronics. And since our trip to the village, I think I would like to look into newspaper work. I still have a year to think it all over," he answered.

"Those both sound like good options," Ms. C. commented.

"And you won't need a lot of history for either one," June pointed out.

"I agree about history," Harry said. "I have trouble with that, too"

"Who wants to be next?" Mr. Hank asked.

"I'm ready," and Shelley stood up. "I'm going to start with something I'm not good at, and that's knitting. I love all the knit things my Mom and my Gramma make. They both knit, and they make lots of lovely things. In the fall and winter they go to craft shows and sell most of what they have made. They love to do it. I sometimes go to the craft fairs with them, and I am truly amazed at some of the things people make-all by hand. I've asked my Mom-and my Gramma- to teach me to knit, and they have both tried a few times, but I just can't seem to get the hang of how those two needles have to work together. When I try to knit each needle wants to go its own way. I'm hopeless. Mom and Gramma have given up on me." Shelley looked dejected.

"As I said before," June spoke up. "You don't have to be good at everything. And speaking of that, what are you good at," she smiled encouragingly.

"Okay! So what I am good at is acting. I just love being in school plays, and reciting at church, and in English class."

"Do you have a lot of things memorized?" Lucy asked hopefully.

"As a matter of fact, I do," Shelley responded happily. "I have memorized a lot of poems that have caught my eye, and scenes from the plays I have been in."

"Would you do some for us sometime?" Ms. C. asked. "I think we would all very much like to hear some."

"Oh, brother!" was heard from Zack.

"Did you have something to add, Zack?" Mr. Hank asked.

"Uh, no! I was, uh, just clearing my throat," Zack said, embarrassed to be the sudden center of attention.

"Okay, continue, Shelley," Mr. Hank prompted.

"Well, that's about it," she said. "I started reciting Bible verses in Sunday school when I was really little, and I just loved doing that. When I started school I always wanted to be in school productions, you know, like on parents night and for the holiday shows? I got really good at it and began to be asked even before tryouts. It's been a lot of fun, too. That's all!"

"That does sound like a lot of fun," Harry said. "I've had parts in a couple of our school plays-not big parts-and it is a lot of fun being in the cast."

"Me, too," June said, "and I agree!"

"Well done, so far. Who's up now?" Ms. C. asked.

"I'm ready," Harry volunteered. "But first I'll show you all my picture frame, and get that out of the way," and he held up a nice looking wooden item about ten inches square with rounded inside edges and corners.

"That's very good, Harry," Mr. Hank said. "Is that your first ever project?"

"Pretty much! I've helped my uncle with some small things around his house, so I've learned to use some of the tools."

"I really like it," June complimented him.

"Thank you! Would you like something like this for your painting?" he offered.

"Are you kidding? I would love it! Would you really do that for me?" June was delighted to get such an offer.

"Sure thing!" Harry smiled. "So, now, what I'm good at is fishing. I know, I know, you're saying to yourselves, 'What's so great about being good at fishing?' Well, let me tell you. Being a good fisherman requires a lot of skill. You have to know quite a bit about fish in the first place. You can't just go to any place with water, and throw a hook in and expect to catch anything-except maybe a cold or an old shoe." Laughter greeted that statement. "Anyway, you also have to have a good rod, and reel. Everybody know what those are?" Harry looked around the group and saw nodding heads, and a few 'Yeses' and 'u' huhs!'

"Okay! Then you have to know in what kind of places fish like to be-especially in brooks and streams. Those are the beautiful places to fish," Harry continued. "Fish prefer shady and cooler places. They don't like the hot sun. You can't always find good places to stand along the banks of brooks and streams, so you need to have a reel that is made for casting-throwing the end of your line further than you can reach. Everyone following me so far?" Again, the nods and 'yeses'.

"Now casting is not as easy as it looks cause you want to get the hook in just the spot you think a fish might be hiding. And then you have to know just how much power you have to throw with to get where you want that hook to land-and that's where the real skill comes in. I've earned a number of awards in fishing contests for good casting and catching." Harry looked around the group again. "And I think that's all," and he took his seat on the log again.

"Hey, just a minute, young man," Mr. Hank said. "You're not out of the hot seat, yet. I think some of us may have questions, and you haven't told us what you're not so good at."

"Uh, sorry about that. I got carried away," and Harry stood up. "Okay, so. Why don't you save any questions or comments 'til I finish. What I'm not good at is taking care of my little brother. He's six years old-quite a bit younger. My dad left us when I was only four or five and my mom didn't remarry until I was ten. So, then along comes this kid. He's not a bad kid, but I just don't know what to do with him when my Mom needs me to 'watch' him. I don't know what I'm supposed to 'watch him' do, and I've forgotten what it's like to be that age. I usually find something on TV and plunk him in front of it. Then I do my homework, or get on the phone with a friend. Mom isn't too happy about that, but…" and he shrugged and sat down.

"What's the biggest fish you have ever caught?" Carl asked.

"Well, in fresh water I once got a three-pound trout. And the one time I went deep sea fishing with my uncle, I caught a thirty-one inch blue fish."

"Fish are pretty smelly, don't ya think?" Zack asked.

"Only if they're out of water too long," Harry quickly replied.

"Which kind of fishing do you like best?" Shelley asked.

"I like fresh water best because I really like woods and streams and lakes. I'm not really crazy about the ocean. I tend to get a little seasick." Harry looked embarrassed to admit that.

"That's nothing to be ashamed off," Mr. Hank sympathized. "When I first joined the navy I was surprised to realize that I was subject to seasickness. I just had to take pills and I was okay, and I finally got used to being on the sea. You could try that if you ever have the chance to go deep sea fishing again." He smiled at Harry, then asked, "And whose turn is it now?"

"Well, I guess I've put it off long enough," June said with a sigh. "First off, here's my painting," and she held up a very fine picture of small pink, white, and purple flowers, surrounded by a few fern and other small greenery.

"Oh, how pretty," Lucy exclaimed. "Where did you see those flowers?"

"Well, I 'imagined' them from a wedding I was in last summer. And the green plants I found in the woods behind the Arts and Crafts building."

"That's a very nice painting, June. You seem to have talent in that direction," Ms. C. praised.

"Thank you both!" June smiled her pleasure at the kind words. "And, now that that's over, I'm also going to start with what I am not good at-get it out of the way. I'm a terrible organizer. I can never figure out what should go where, or in what order things should be done. When I DO straighten up my room-when my mother tells me to for the fourth time-I can't remember-for days-where I put anything, and don't find some things for weeks. Being disorganized is such a time waster, and I annoy myself as much as I do others, but..."and June shrugged her shoulders.

"I have that trouble, too," Shelley commiserated.

June thanked Shelley with a smile. "Okay, now for the good stuff! I am a really good cheerleader. I started in junior high school. I had taken gymnastics when I was in grade school, so I had some experience. But most gymnastics you do by yourself, not in a team. That was the hardest part for me-getting the timing right with the rest of the squad. But now I'm the leader. And I'll miss it terribly when I graduate."

"Wow! That's great!" Carl congratulated her. "We have a good cheering squad at our school, too!"

"Can you do a real split and backwards somersault, too?" Lucy asked.

"Yep! I learned those in gymnastics, so I was all set there. I think building the pyramids are the most difficult for me. I'm okay on the bottom, but nowhere else."

"That's a very important position-no bottom-no top," Harry said philosophically. And everyone laughed.

"Well, it looks like you're up now, Zack. I think you also have a fine piece of art work to show us first?" Ms. C. queried.

"Uh, yes, I do!" Now that he was in the spotlight Zack was very nervous, no snappy remarks, no bravado. "Here it is!" And he held up a wooden frame, similar to Harry's in size, but beautifully decorated with intricate carvings.

"How beautiful, Zack," Mr. Hank commented as he studied the delicate designs on the frame. "You must do a lot of carving. These figures are very fine."

"Um, yes I do a lot of whittling-carving I guess is a better word, but I started whittling-you know-sticks I picked up in the grass. My Oldman-uh, father, gave me a little pocket knife when I was just about eight. I spent a lot of time by myself, and I'd have my pocket knife and there'd be sticks, all kinds, and I'd make marks in them and shave little strips off them. One thing led to another, and I learned how to make designs on them. It passed the time." Zack had given this little speech to the ground at his feet. Now he looked up to see that the whole group had been listening carefully to all he had to say.

"You do beautiful wood carving, Zack," Ms. C.'s praise seemed genuine, but Zack was suspicious, too many people say nice things just 'cause they are supposed to.

"I told him his was way better than mine, didn't I Zack?" Harry chimed in.

"Yeah, yeah! So what! It's just something I do to pass the time-no big deal," Zack was really uncomfortable with all the silence from the other kids, and the attention they were paying him. He'd had enough.

"Okay, so, on to what I don't do so well. As if you all haven't figured it out already, it's I don't make many friends," and he looked around at his camp mates. They could almost see the chip on his shoulder.

"Maybe it's your shining personality," June offered.

"No sarcasm, please," Ms. C. said warningly.

"We're your friends, Zack," Lucy said.

"Yeah, but only 'cause you have to be-in camp. If we met on the street you'd walk by like you didn't even know me. I been there and I know." Zack's face was getting very red. He looked close to tears.

"Hey, I don't think me and Lucy have told you guys about the bear we saw by the lake today," Carl nearly shouted. Things were getting a little scary.

"You did not see a bear," Shelley said, feigning disbelief, hoping to break the tension, though Lucy had already told June and her about the critter.

"Oh, yes we did!" Lucy played along.

"Where was it?" Harry asked-truly not having heard the story as yet.

"Well, we were canoeing along, close to the shore. There's a place where the forest comes out into the lake. We went around that and there it was, taking a drink by a huge rock. We didn't make any noise and the bear didn't seem to notice us at all. We didn't go any closer, and then it stood up, sniffed the air and went back into the woods. It was awesome." Carl had everyone's attention as he told the story.

"Wow! I would've liked to see that," Harry said.

"Well, maybe that ole bear will hang around for a bit and we will be able to see it on our cave hunting hike tomorrow," Mr. Hank announced. That got everyone's attention pretty quickly.

"Can we really?" asked an excited Shelley.

"I don't see why not--if Lucy thinks she is up for it?" and Ms. C. looked questioningly at her.

"Me? I'm great! I'm up for," and she paused, "well, for pretty much anything," she amended. "My ankle isn't bothering me very much at all, and Nurse Kathy can give it a wrap just to be on the safe side."

"Okay, then that's our plan," Mr. Hank continued. "We will leave just after breakfast and have the Dining Hall crew put up bag lunches for us. Okay?"

"Oh, boy!" Carl exclaimed. "We're gonna look for those caves I'm pretty sure I saw on our mountain hike, aren't we, Mr. Hank?"

"Yep, that's the idea. Then we will know for sure. Right now, I think it's just about bed time. So, good night all! Rest well, and see you in the morning," he said with finality.

"Beth," he addressed Ms. C. as the kids all headed to their cabins, "I'm going to check in with Matt and let him know our plans for tomorrow."

"Good idea!" she said. "See you in the morning!"

Mr. Hank enjoyed his stroll in the quiet of the evening under the brilliantly lit sky, full of stars, and a very big moon-to the office, where he found Matt doing more of the unending paperwork.

"Hi, Hank, grab a chair. I'm just about finished here for the day," Matt greeted him.

"Thanks, Matt. Don't let me interrupt you! I can wait," Hank assured him.

"Not a problem! I was going to have a staff meeting in the morning. I had a visit from Officer Kettering today. He had some news that I think we all need to know," he continued. "You remember those animal poachers we had around here last summer, causing so much trouble?"

"Hard to forget them. I thought they were locked away for a few years," he said.

"Oh, yeah! They're still behind bars, but, it seems there are two strange dudes who have been hanging around in town. They've been there for a couple days, and have been asking around about caves in the area. Officer Kettering stopped in to update me,....."

"Why does he think that's necessary?" Hank interrupted. "Have they asked about the Retreat?" Hank didn't like the sound of what he was hearing.

"I'm getting to that," Matt explained. "It seems they have asked about where the Retreat is located. One of them said he had a 'friend' who had spent some time around here last year. Officer Kettering got very suspicious when he heard that. He called up to the prison. He asked if our two poachers had had any visitors lately. He confirmed that the one named Buck had, indeed, had a recent visitor. He signed in as 'Gene Wilder, aka 'Guy'. This 'friend' doesn't have a record that the warden could find. But that doesn't mean he doesn't have one."

"I definitely don't like the sound of that," Hank was quite disturbed with this news. "Me and Beth have just promised the kids a hike tomorrow to see if we can find a possible cave in the hills just east of here, up on Mount Gregory. A few days ago, when we were coming back from our mountain hike, one of my boys thought he saw a spot across the valley that looked like it might be hiding a cave. At the time I said we might take a hike over there to find out one day. Then Lucy had her accident, and that hike got postponed. Now Lucy is back in good shape and we just made the plan for tomorrow. The kids are really looking forward to it, and I don't want to disappoint them." Hank slumped back in the chair.

"Now, just because some stranger is asking around about caves, is no reason you should postpone your hike." Matt reasoned.

"I know. But I just don't like the sound of it all. We surely don't want to put the kids in harm's way," Hank was clearly worried.

"Okay! I understand. Let's give Officer Kettering a call and see if he has any further information about the activities of these two guys."

Matt immediately picked up the phone. In just a moment he had Officer Kettering on the line. He explained Hank's concerns.

"Well, these guys have mostly been hanging around the town. I've seen them every day, one place or another. They have been talking to a lot of the old timers-asking about trails and caves-things like that," he said.

"Do you know if they have gotten any specifics-any definite trail to take, any particular cave's location-things like that?" Matt pressed him.

"Not that I've heard, but I haven't really investigated that deeply. Officer Blackwell and I can check around some more tomorrow. How's that?" he asked.

Matt relayed the information to Hank. "Can you hold off for another day?" he asked.

"I'd really rather not. The kids have been waiting for Lucy to get better and now that she is, and is also rearing to go, it just might take the wind out of their sails-be a really big disappointment." Hank sighed, and looked thoughtful. "And, I guess, there isn't very strong evidence of a real problem. I don't know how I would explain it to them without causing more upset. I'll let Beth know what's going on and we can both be extra vigilant."

Hank had held the phone between them so Officer Kettering could hear them both. "What do you think, Officer Kettering?"

"At this time, I don't think we have to push the panic button," he answered. "You and the kids go ahead. I'll let Rangers Brown and Curtis know what your plans are, where you expect to be tomorrow. Let's see what Officer Blackwell and I can find out tomorrow. How does that sound?"

"Like a good plan," Hank agreed. "I feel better knowing that the proper authorities will be looking out for us as well." Hank stood up and turned to leave. "Thanks, Matt! We'll see you at breakfast. And thanks to you, too, Officer Kettering," he called out, loud enough to be heard over the phone that Matt was preparing to hang up.

CHAPTER EIGHT

The next morning dawned with a lovely sunrise, and a cloudless sky. The Unit Three kids needed little prompting to get up and get off to breakfast so their new adventure could begin.

"Hurry up and get dressed, girls. I'm going over to the Dining Hall and get our table. I also want to make sure the staff knows we'll be wanting bag lunches. See you over there. Put a wiggle on!" And Ms. C. was out the door.

"What are you going to wear?" Lucy asked Shelley. "What's good for hiking and cave exploring?"

"I can't answer about exploring caves 'cause I've never done that. As for the hiking, you remember when we went up the mountain and you fell down it?" She couldn't resist joking about that with Lucy.

"Yeah, yeah, so I was a stumble bum. But I'm back to being perfect now," she joked back. "And I know we had to wear long pants, and have a sweater or light weight jacket 'cause it gets colder the higher you get. We should probably dress pretty much the same cause a cave could get pretty cold without any sunshine. What do you think?"

"Sounds good to me," came from June who was just coming back from the bath house. "It's a really beautiful day. We should have a super time. I'm very looking forward to it. Let's get going. We don't want the boys to think we're lazy, do we?"

"We most certainly don't," Lucy said. "I'm just about ready. And don't forget, we should wear bright colors so we'll be easy to see amongst all the greenery."

"That's in case we get lost," Shelley added. "I don't think anyone is planning on getting lost, do you?"

"But you never know," June said. "I'm sure Lucy never expected the mountain to fall apart on her on our last hike, did you, Lucy?"

"I sure didn't, but everything turned out alright, and I got to know Carl real well. He's a real good guy." Lucy paused a moment in her dressing, and gave a sigh, "I'll miss him when we have to go home."

"We still have quite a few more days left, more than a week and a lot can happen in that time. So, let's just enjoy each day as it comes. Okay?" Shelley advised.

"That's the best way!" June agreed. "Hurry up! I'm ready!" And she pushed through the door.

"So am I," Shelley and Lucy chorused, and raced after her.

The boys had beaten them to the Dining Hall and had already filled their plates.

"We saved some for you," Harry assured them as they got to the table.

"There are some delicious biscuits this morning," Carl said, and plunked his over laden plate down on the table.

Zack didn't say anything, just sort of grumbled as he shoveled a forkful of scrambled eggs into his mouth.

"Good morning to you, too, Zack" Lucy said, tossing a smile his way.

"I'm eatin'. I don't talk with my mouth full," and another forkful disappeared.

"Now we're all here. Let's finish breakfast as quickly as we can-without gobbling everything, that is," Mr. Hank advised. "This hike will be a bit longer than our other mountain one, but some of it will be on flatter land, so we should be able to move right along."

The girls got in line and, were soon back at the table with plates loaded with their favorites. There was little further chatter as everyone ate their fill.

No more than fifteen minutes later everyone was finished. Ms. C. stood up. "It looks like we are all finished here. The staff have our bagged lunches and water bottles ready, and we can pick them up on the front porch, so let's go!"

Mr. Hank led them out. "Just grab a lunch, and a water bottle, stash them in your packs, and then gather round me when you have them-and don't forget to thank the staff," he reminded them. They were soon all gathered. "Okay! First off-do you all have your flashlights? If we do find any caves, they will most likely not have electricity."

There was some laughter at that, and many 'Yeses, Yeps,' and nodded heads answered.

"That's good! So, the area we want to investigate is east of here," and he pointed to the mountains behind him. "I have a good map that has a well-marked trail. To get there we are going to go through the Retreat. The trail doesn't look very difficult, just long, so we will have a rest stop or two. If anyone has any problem-shoes are uncomfortable, toes hurt, getting a blister, please let me or Ms. C. know right away. We don't want small problems to become big problems. We have a first aid kit-and just a reminder, for your future adventures-never go hiking without a basic first aid kit-and can solve most small problems quite easily. Any questions?"

"What if someone wants to come back here in the middle of the hike?" Zack asked.

"I would say that if anyone thinks-right now-that that might happen, they should say so-right now, and we can hook them up with another Unit for the day. Does anyone think that?" and his eyes scanned the group, and then went back to Zack.

"Well, I was just saying," Zack shrugged his shoulders, and stared at the dirt at his feet.

"Any other questions?" There were none. "Okay, let's hit the trail," And Mr. Hank set off with a brisk stride. The kids fell in line behind him, Harry, then Zack, followed by Shelley and June. Carl, who was still feeling protective of Lucy, was walking right behind her at the end of the little group-just in case she might need some help along the way, with Ms. C. bringing up the rear-as was usual, though it wasn't necessary to go single file yet. It didn't take long for them to pass through the sunny Retreat grounds. They went past the Arts and Crafts Building, bypassed the tennis courts, went around the barn, and skirted the ropes course. Then the forest closed in, and the way was shaded.

"Thank goodness for the shade," June said, and took out her handkerchief-which was really a large bandana.

"Wherever did you get that?" Lucy asked. "I'd like one."

"We have a hiking club at our school, and we all have these because they can be used for many things-like a sling for a broken arm, a wrap for a twisted ankle, a head covering if the sun is too hot-just lots of things," June explained. "I didn't have it the day you had your fall, but it wouldn't have been much help for your injuries anyway."

"That's okay! I'll look for one when I get back home-for the next time," Lucy replied.

The trail narrowed just then and it was single file for a while. The forest sounds provided soft background accompaniment to the chatter of the kids. The group had been moving along at a moderate pace when Lucy suddenly stopped and bent down over a patch of blossoms. "Oh, look at these little white flowers. I wonder what they are. Do you know the name of these flowers, Ms. C.?" she asked.

Ms. C. moved up beside her and scooched down to get a better look at the clump of green and white beauty. "No, I'm afraid I don't, Lucy. Botany wasn't one of the required classes for my degree," she answered. "I'm pretty sure there is a book about local flora at the office. Next hike we take we must remember to bring it. But we can take a look when we get back, and maybe we will find it in there, okay?"

"Yeah! I'll try to keep its picture in my head," she promised.

"Good! And now we better hurry! The other guys are getting way ahead of us," Ms. C. advised.

They picked up their pace and soon caught up. The trail was getting a bit more rugged. It wound around large boulders, and between trees of all sizes. At one spot a gurgling brook flowed across their path, singing a happy tune as it flowed on its way. Mr. Hank called a rest stop just there. It was a very pleasant place, and they had been on their way for nearly an hour.

"Take a break and a drink of water." Mr. Hank directed. It's important to stay hydrated when you're hiking."

"Yeah! And when you're doing sports," Carl added. "We were told that in soccer," he said.

"We heard that at cheerleading as well," June agreed.

"Getting dehydrated isn't a good thing to happen to anyone at any time," Ms. C. said. "And when you are being physically active your body needs a lot of water. So, drink up gang," and she took a big swallow from her own water bottle.

Ten minutes or so later Mr. Hank said, "Okay, let's get back on the trail. The going is getting a little steeper now. Be aware of loose rocks," he cautioned. "And I'm hoping we may see some wildlife up here. There are deer all over these forests, but they are very shy, and leap away at the smallest sound. So let's be really quiet-which isn't that easy to do when you are stepping on sticks and rocks, but we can try." He slung his pack over his shoulder and started off up the mountain trail once again. One by one the kids resumed their places, Ms. C. again at the end of the line.

Onward and slightly upward they trod. Occasionally, Harry could hear muttered complaints from behind him. He paid little attention to them. It was just Zack-being Zack. It was hard enough for Zack to find pleasure from ordinary everyday happenings, so it was no big surprise that he was having trouble finding any in this challenging mountain hike. For Harry, it was a delight-being outdoors in clear mountain air, with the sighing of the gently swaying pine boughs, and the warming sunshine. "Poor Zack," he thought. "He just doesn't know how to be happy. Poor guy."

There were a few places when the mountain became gentler, seemed to level out, and the going got easier. "This is a little more challenging than I thought it would be," June said to no one in particular."

"Yeah, I think so, too," Shelley agreed. "But it is such a beautiful day. The air is so clear, and the sky is so blue. You can hear the birds twittering.…."

"Shhh! Everyone stop, and be very quiet," came a whispered order from Mr. Hank who had his arms out as if to hold them back as he lowered himself into a crouch. After a minute or two he began to motion them forward. One by one they crept slowly to where he knelt behind a wide, bushy shrub. "Look over the bush, not to fast, easy does it," he warned as each one crawled close. "Oh, my goodness," Shelley breathed out. "That is sooo beautiful!"

"What? What?" June asked. "I can't see any….Oh! Oh! Now I see." She stopped short, gazing in awe at the unexpected sight. "I never thought I would ever see a deer and baby in the wild."

"I seen lots of them on television. What's the big deal?" Zack pretty much sneered, which got him a black look from Carl, who had just gotten to the bush with Lucy.

"Don't pay any attention to him," he told Lucy. "Take a peek, Lucy, just there over the bush and to the right."

"Oh, wow! They are beautiful. And look, there are two babies," as at that moment a second fawn stepped into the clearing from the shade of the woods. "Twins! They are sooooo cute," Lucy barely dared breathe.

"It's a real treat to see such a sight," Ms. C. said as she took her own peek over the bush. "And a rare one, too. We are very lucky today. This is only the third time I have seen such a sight and I have lived in this area for the last four years."

"Yes, I have lived here for some time as well, and this is, indeed, an unusual occurrence," Mr. Hank agreed. They watched quietly as the mother deer slowly moved across the clearing with her babies galumphing along at her side on their spindly, little legs.

"Oh, there they go," Shelley said as mom and babies disappeared into the forest. "That was truly awesome!"

Zack had his own comment, "You can see all the animals you want, any time you want, at the zoo."

"Zack, how about you keep your comments to yourself," Carl said.

"Okay, boys! Be respectful! Let's get back to our hike! We must be pretty near where you thought you saw the cave, don't you think, Carl?" Mr. Hank asked as he, along with the others, stood and stretched.

Carl turned in a small circle, looking at all the mountains that surrounded them. Then he pointed at a particular summit across the valley. "Is that the mountain we hiked the other day?" he asked him.

"Yep, that's the one! What do you think?" Mr. Hank repeated.

"Yeah! We must be pretty close-maybe up just a bit more?" he said questioningly.

"Okay gang, we'll go on up a ways and see what's there-maybe another fifteen minutes-and then it will be lunch time as well. How's that?"

"Oh, goody!" from Zack, which earned him scowl from Ms. C., to which Zack shrugged his shoulders.

"Sounds like a plan," Harry agreed.

"Then let's get a move on," June said, and started up the rough trail.

Just about fifteen minutes later, the group reached a spot of fairly open ground which was backed by a jumble of huge boulders. The boulders looked like they had been thrown down higgledy-piggledy by some fantastic giant.

"Let's stop here," Mr. Hank said. "There's plenty of room for us all to spread out and have lunch."

Everyone unloaded their backpacks and settled comfortably on the scrubby grass or on a handy rock. "I'm starving," Shelley commented, and took a huge bite out of her sandwich.

"Me, too," and Harry did the same.

For some minutes, not much conversation could be heard as all dug into their packs and hungrily attacked their thoughtfully prepared meal.

"That hit the spot. Let's be sure we don't leave any litter behind," Ms. C. reminded them, as she stuck her empty wrappings into her own pack.

"Hey, does anyone want to do some rock climbing? These huge boulders are awesome," Carl said. He was studying the huge pile of stone. "They look like they could have been what I saw the other day." While he was talking, he was walking to the base of the pile, where the mountain slope, crowded with tall pines, hid the valley from view.

"I'm game," Harry said, and joined Carl by the rock pile.

"Me, too," June said.

"Let's not be too hasty," Mr. Hank cautioned as he surveyed the size of the obstacle in front of them. "Let's see what they look like from the other side first. Okay?"

"Right, that's a good idea," Harry agreed.

With Mr. Hank in the lead, the four of them squeezed between the bottom of one of the mammoth boulders and the trunk of a mighty pine that looked like it was hugging the rock.

"Hey! Wait for us," Lucy called out, and she and Shelley hurried over.

"What do you think, Zack?" asked Ms. C. "Do you want to join in?"

"Naw! Rocks ain't one of my things," he answered.

"Okay! We can wait here then," and she settled her against a fallen tree.

It didn't take long for the last of the group to disappear around the huge hump of stone. Then, soon thereafter, came an excited whoop of glee, "It's here! It's here! Come see! You have to come see, Zack, Ms. C. You have to see for yourself," June's voice called out.

Ms. C. looked at Zack, who had sat up straighter at the sound of the excited voice. "It sounds like there is something extraordinary on the other side, Zack. Let's go, shall we? We don't want to miss something really great!"

"Oh, all right, if I have to," but Ms. C. could see from his expression he was getting interested.

"Okay! We're coming!" she called back.

It was a tight squeeze through that particular spot, which had not been made any easier by all the others who had already gone ahead, but in just minutes they were standing with the others, staring into the partially opened mouth of a mountain cave. Some forest greenery was dangling above the opening, obscuring some of the interior.

"It doesn't look like this cave has been visited recently," Mr. Hank observed. "The soil and brush around the entrance look undisturbed."

"Do you think there might be a bear in there?" Shelley asked in a hushed voice.

"Don't ya think if there was, it would be looking back at us after June's screaming?" Zack said.

"Okay, so maybe that was a stupid question, but..."

"No, Shelley," interrupted Mr. Hank. "At this time of year, you won't usually find a bear in its cave. It will be out hunting food, constantly," he assured them. "The only things you are most likely to find in there would be bats, spiders and other insects. It's also unlikely, but possible, that some other kind of animal could have crawled in there," he added.

"I wonder how big it is inside," Carl said. "Anyone want to go in?" he asked, and searched the faces of his friends. "Isn't anyone brave enough to go in with me?" No one stepped forward. "Com'on! It's a once in a life time opportunity," he implored.

"Actually, I think I'd like to do a little exploring," Harry said. "We don't have to go in very far-just take a look......"

"I'm game," June said.

"OKaaaay!" Harry looked as surprised at her remark as Carl felt-a girl in a dark and spooky cave? He shrugged his shoulders. "Yeah, whatever! The more the merrier!"

"We'll wait right out here," Lucy assured them. "You better be back in no more than fifteen minutes, or we'll send in a search party."

"Year! Yeah! We won't get lost," Harry called back. "Hard to do that in a place like this-one way in and one way out," he reminded her. "Let's go then! We can do this," and he boldly walked to the cave's mouth. "Anyone in here?" he shouted.

Only a small echo answered him.

"Nope, on one's at home," and he pushed though the opening with Carl right behind, and June gamely following. Daylight followed them only a short distance before the dark began to take over.

Just then Lucy hollered in: "Hey, you guys! What about flashlights?"

Carl looked sheepishly at Harry, who was looking the same back at him. "Duh!" Carl said.

"Yeah! Right!" Harry agreed.

"I'll go get 'em for us," June offered. "I'll be right back," and she hurried back to the entrance.

Carl and Harry backtracked a bit towards the light, studying the high ceiling and walls as they went. There was no cave art work to be seen, just rubble on the cave floor, some cobwebs here and there, and wet marks running from ceiling to floor.

"Here you are, guys! I got mine, too. Let's do this!" June said as she reentered the cave, holding out the flashlights, and looking very determined to stay with them.

"Thanks, June!" Carl said, and they turned around and headed further into the cavern, their flashlights leading the way into the gloom.

"This all looks pretty tame, not scary at all," Harry commented.

"At least that's how it looks now," Carl reminded him. "There's a lot more to explore here than meets the eye, I'm thinking." Indeed, the cave was beginning to widen out, and the ceiling was receding upwards. The flashlights revealed tall columns extending down from the ceiling, and others rising up from the floor.

"Oh, wow!" June was awestruck. "I think these are the stalactites and the stalagmites I read about in my beginning course in geology," she exclaimed with excitement in her voice.

"What are? You mean these columns?" Carl asked as he stared in wonder.

"If I remember it correctly, the stalactites are the ones coming down from the ceiling, and the stalagmites grow up from the floor, you know, from all the dripping from the ceiling," June explained.

"Well, they are just awesome, is all I can say-whatever they're called," he responded.

"Hey, you guys! What's happening in there?" Shelley called out, her voice sounding hollow in the depth of the cave.

"Com'on in and see for yourselves," June called back. "You really don't want to miss this."

"Okay! You've talked us into it. Here we come!" Lucy's excited voice bounced off the stone walls.

Five more flashlights soon added their glow to the ambiance of the cave, highlighting the sparkles of the tites and mites.

"Wow! Look at this. It's magical!" Shelley breathed out, barely above a whisper.

"It looks like a cathedral in here," Lucy said.

Zack had yet to say anything. He had never seen anything remotely like this-ever. For once he had no smart-aleky remarks to make. He let his flashlight roam over the fabulous formations from top to bottom-truly awestruck.

"This definitely is a 'Wow'," Mr. Hank said to Ms. C. "This will have to be a regular hiking trip for our campers, now that we have discovered this wondrous cave, don't you think?"

"Absolutely," she responded. "What a perfect adventure!"

Meanwhile, Carl, Harry, and June had begun to venture further into the depths of this marvelous cavern.

"Is that another cave opening there on the right?" June asked, training her light on a dark area on the side wall. "It looks like it might be," she added as she cautiously followed her light. The boys were close behind her.

"It sure looks like it," Carl said as they got closer.

"Yep, it is, but not a very large one," Harry bent down to look into this new opening. His flashlight illuminated the solid end of the small cave not more than five feet in. "Not very big for sure. Let's see if there are any more," he urged.

"Yes, let's," June agreed, enthusiastically.

"Yeah! Lucy, we're going looking for side caves. Wan'na come?" Carl called to her.

"Not right now! I'm really interested in how these stalac… things are made. You go ahead. Catch ya' later!" was her reply.

"Okay! Later!" and he was off.

The rest of the members of the little group dispersed to explore on their own.

Suddenly, "Oh, my!" was heard with an echoing sound from across the length of the cave. "Look at that!" Shelley exclaimed.

"What? What? Where are you?" Lucy called out.

"Over here! I'm waving my flashlight! Can you see it?" Shelley called back.

"Okay, I see it! I'm coming," she answered. "Carl, where are you?"

"I see your light, too, Shelley, and I'm on my way. Meet you there, Lucy," he responded.

"I'm on my way, as well," Ms. C. chimed in. "Sounds like something quite exciting."

Pretty soon all seven other flashlights were converging on Shelley's location. Zack was the first to arrive. "What's up, Shel…? Oh…….!" At this point Zack became speechless. All he could do is stop and stare at the spotlight shining on Shelley. Then he looked up and saw the blue sky, a wisp of white cloud, and a small shaft of sunshine coming through a wide gap in the roof overhead, surrounded by a frame of jagged rock. Who knew! Apparently, there was a back door to this cavern, and it was high above. One by one they were joined by the others.

"Well, look at that will you!" Mr. Hank stood staring upwards with a look of wonder on his face.

"Do you think we could climb up there?" Zack asked?

Mr. Hank turned in a tight circle, examining all the rocky walls between them and the hole in the sky. "It looks pretty rugged to me," he said. "And we don't have any of the right equipment to even begin to try."

"Maybe we can find it from the top," Zack suggested.

"Not today, I'm afraid," Ms. C. said. "It's getting late. Pretty soon we will have to start back, and it's a good hike back to the Retreat. We can save that for another day-something to look forward to."

"Oh, goody!" came from Zack. "Just when something really interesting happens."

"Zack, we have had a fine hike and a fine day, but the day is moving along, and, so must we-very soon. Okay?" Mr. Hank explained. "There's always another day," and he patted Zack's shoulder.

So, for the next quarter hour or so, the kids and counsellors continued their exploration of this, heretofore, unknown treasure. Nothing else extraordinary was discovered except three more, much smaller, side caves, one of which had a couple lumpy humps in it. Worried that they might be sleeping animals, they were left undisturbed. By this time flashlights were beginning to dim, and the explorers to feel the chill of the underground.

"Okay, kids! It's getting late! Time to head back," Ms. C.'s voice echoed around and through the giant columns made by Mother Nature.

"And we need to find our way out of this cave while we still have some flashlight left," agreed Mr. Hank. He and Ms. C. waited for all the kids to gather around before heading to the cave's entrance, and the warmth of the outside.

"That was truly awesome." Lucy said as the group emerged into the mid-afternoon sun. "I don't think I shall ever forget it."

"Me neither," agreed Shelley.

"I wish I had a camera," June said. "Hey, Carl, "if we can come back another time with a camera would you take some pictures for us?"

"Sure, I would! I don't know a lot about taking pictures in such a dark place, but I can try," he said. "That would be great! And a picture of that hole in the roof-maybe from the other side of it. Yeah!" He was excited at the prospect.

"And you can take some pictures of us all outside the entrance." Lucy enthused.

"Yes, then we would all have a great souvenir of this fine adventure," Harry added.

"I don't need no picture to remember this place," Zack said.

"Well, regardless kids, it's a good hike back down the mountain, and the day is moving on, and so must we," Ms. C. reminded them.

"Okay! So take a drink of your water, and we'll get on down the hill," Mr. Hank directed. "And watch your step for loose stones and dirt as you go down-no more accidents! Okay?"

A chorus of "Yes, sir's," were heard, and the group got moving, chatting among themselves about what they had seen, especially that hole in the roof. It was agreed that it sure would be exciting to come back and investigate that more closely.

The hike back was uneventful, and went more quickly than the upward climb had. They were all happy to reach level ground again. Fortunately, they arrived just as dinner was being served in the Dining Hall. A side trip to the cabin to unload backpacks, and to the bath house for a quick wash up, and they sat down to the usual, very satisfying, meal that the professional kitchen staff prepared each night. Tomorrow was another day to be filled with activities that would be fun, educational, challenging, and shared with others they were coming to know, and whose company they liked. Indeed-something to look forward to!

CHAPTER NINE

The next morning the sky was cloudy, warning of some rain before nightfall. After breakfast, the kids went off to their favorite activities: June and Lucy to the Arts and Crafts building; Shelley to the lake for another swimming lesson; Carl to find interesting things to photograph in the different lighting of the overcast sky; and Harry and Zack to woodworking.

"I didn't get a chance to talk with Matt yesterday evening about our hike," Hank told Beth. "I'm going to the office to do that now. Want to come along?"

"Sure! I have some paperwork to catch up on there," she said. "And I can join your conversation."

It was a good time to see Matt, as he had just come out onto the porch to greet Officers Kettering and Blackwell. "These officers have come with an update on the two strangers in town who had been asking around about caves and trails," he said as he introduced Hank and Beth. "These are the counsellors for the kids that went hiking yesterday," he explained

"Nice to meet you," Officer Kettering stuck out his hand to shake with Hank, and he nodded to Beth, who greeted him and Officer Blackwell with a smile.

"Nice to meet you as well," Hank said. "We've come to tell Matt of our mountain adventure yesterday."

"And it has to do with caves and trails," Beth added.

"Let's go into my office. We can talk better there." When they were all seated, Matt asked, "What have you been able to learn about our two strangers?"

Officer Kettering took the lead. "Well, we had the name of the guy who went to see Buck up at the prison. 'Gene Wilder' aka 'Guy'. At first look, no record showed up for him, but when we dug a little deeper, it seems he has a record out in Oregon. He was caught hunting illegally out there. He was only fined on the first offense, but when they suspected him again, they couldn't find him. We sent his picture up to the prison, and they verified it was one of our strangers."

"We haven't been able to find out much about his buddy here," Officer Blackwell spoke up, "just his name, Bill Hardy aka 'Willy'. We don't have a local record on him, but we'll keep looking," she assured them.

"Wait a minute!" Matt said. "I remember hearing something about a cache of furs from the rangers. They heard about it from Maria, the camper who was kidnapped by those two thugs last summer. She said she heard them talking about 'a stash of skins they had in a cave'. As far as I know, no such stash has ever been found."

"I think we need to get in touch with those rangers," Officer Kettering said, "get their take on things-find out what has been done regarding any 'stash'."

"I'll see if I can get them on the line right now," and Matt picked up his phone and began to dial. He put it on speaker. After a moment, "Hello, this is Matt Prada, at Tuckaway Retreat. I'd like to speak with Ranger Brown or Curtis if possible."

"This is Ranger Brown, Mr. Prada. Is everything all right at the Retreat? We haven't heard from you folks for a while. And you're on speaker phone."

"Same here, and we are doing fine, but something a little disconcerting has happened," and he went on to explain the situation. "And we are wondering if any stashes of skins or furs have been found in any caves in the area. Our town strangers-at least one of them-seem to be connected to last year's bad guys, and they may be looking for any such stashes."

"As far as I know," Ranger Brown said, "no such stash has been recovered. We did go out searching in the caves we know about. But there are a lot of mountains around here, and caves can be hard to find. They get covered over with all the trees and other vegetation."

"We found a cave yesterday," Beth spoke up. "Our hike was up on Mount Gregory. We got pretty near the top. There was a huge bundle of boulders, and, when we rounded them, we found a fair sized cave."

"Yes, that's right!" and Hank took over the story. "The opening was partially screened with greenery, but inside it opened up considerably. It went deeply into the mountain-stalactites and stalagmites galore. There were a few much small caverns along the sides. And there was even a back entrance high up in the roof, letting in some light."

"Well, that's some find," Ranger Curtis said. She spoke to Ranger Brown. "We'll have to take a hike up there ourselves one of these days and get those caves checked out. We need to have them on our maps as well. We need to know about all such places. They would be attractive to hikers, as well as wildlife."

"You're right about that. And we need to know it as a place to look if there are ever any lost hikers in the area," Ranger Brown added.

"Okay!" Officer Kettering broke in. "So we all know a little more now. Here in town we will keep a better watch on our visitors, and there on the reserve you guys can be on the watch as well. We can send over the picture we have of Gene Wilder. We are still working on the other guy, Bill Hardy and let you know as soon as, and 'if', we get anything on him. How's that?"

"Sounds like a plan," Ranger Brown agreed.

"Well then, I think that's all we can do here," Officer Blackwell said as she stood up. "We need to get back into town. We will keep you all apprised of any developments, and ask you to do the same. We surely don't want a repeat of last year's situation."

"Yes, and we thank you all very much for your assistance and care. It is much appreciated," Matt assured them, as he hung up the phone and stood to see the officers to the door.

"Beth and I are heading back to the Unit, Matt. Thanks for including us in the conversation," Hank said. "I hope that is the last we will have to do with any stranger and 'skins'."

"I'll second that," Beth said with a smile. "Let's go see how the kids did this morning, Hank. See you later, Matt!" Paperwork was forgotten for the moment.

"Yeah! Thanks for coming in," and, with a wave, Matt went back to his desk.

"Do you think there is anything to be concerned about, Hank?" Beth asked with a worried look.

"No, I don't, now that the officers **and** the rangers are aware of a possible connection with last year's situation," he replied. "It's is strange, though."

"Well, there's no use worrying. We can't do anything more," and Beth lapsed into a thoughtful silence as they neared their cabins. "Oh, for goodness sake. I forgot I wanted to catch up on some paperwork. I'll see you later, Hank," and she turned to retrace her steps back to the administration building.

Some of the kids had finished with their morning activities and were sitting on the rocks and logs around the fire pit outside the girls cabin when Hank arrived. "Hello everyone," Hank called out in greeting. "I see we are missing two of us."

"Yeah," June said. "I'm pretty sure Shelley is most likely still splashing around up at the lake. She's really excited about her swimming progress."

"I caught sight of Carl down at the sport field with his camera stuff," Harry offered.

"June and I had fun trying out painting with oil paint," Lucy said. "It seems stickier than water colors, and, of course, you have to be careful not to splash it around-hard to get out of your clothes. The brushes need more cleaning, too," she added.

"Duh! That's why it's called 'oil' paint," Zack muttered.

"Zack, do you ever think of good things to say?" June asked him with a frown on her face.

"What's the matter with what I said? I was just pointing out the obvious," he answered. "What's it to you, anyhow?"

"Hey, kids! I don't like what I'm hearing. You all know our camp rules of kindness and courtesy. You don't have to agree with each other, but you **do** have to show respect," Mr. Hank was very unhappy with what he was observing. "I think apologies are in order," he said staring at Zack.

"Why is it always me getting singled out?" he whined. "I'm entitled to my opinions, ain't I, just like everybody else?"

"Of course you are! But your manner of expressing them needs some adjustment. Have you ever heard, 'It's not what you say, but how you say it?'" Mr. Hank continued, still focusing on Zack.

"What the heck! I don't do anything right according to you all." Zack turned and stalked off into the surrounding trees, anger evident in the set of his shoulders.

"When you come back, be prepared to apologize," Mr. Hank called after him. "Okay, kids! Did you all have good mornings?" he asked, just as Carl came walking into the area, looking at something in his camera, and nearly tripping over the end of the log Harry was sitting on.

"Huh! What's up? Where's Zack going?" he asked, looking at Zack's retreating back.

"Just for a cooling down stroll," Harry said. "And, yes, Mr. Hank, Zack and I had a good time at woodworking. We are learning how to cut different kinds of corners and details for making boxes. It was very challenging and interesting." He hoped his comments helped settle the awkward situation.

"Hey, everybody! You all waiting for me?" Shelley called out as she came into the clearing. "The lifeguard, Peter, told me I'm doing really good. I tried diving, too-but that didn't go so well. He said what I did was more of a belly-flop-I guess cause if you do it wrong, you mostly end up falling on your belly, and that's a big 'ouch'."

"I'm sure you'll get the hang of it next time, Shelley," Lucy assured her.

Just then Ms. C. arrived. "Hey, all! It's just about lunch time. Everybody hungry? And where's Zack?" she said looking around the fire circle.

"He'll probably meet us at the Dining Hall," Mr. Hank told her.

"I'll catch up with you all, too. I need to return this camera to the photo shop," Carl said, and headed down the same trail Zack had taken.

He increased his pace, hoping to catch up with his camp mate. "Hey, Zack! Wait up! Where're you going?" he asked when he came even.

"What do you care? No one will miss me anyhow," was Zack's reply.

"What's the matter?" Carl asked quietly.

"Oh, the usual, my unwelcome comments."

"Well, you do come out with some off the wall statements," Carl had to admit.

"I just say what I'm thinking. What's the matter with that?" Zack argued.

"I know you don't mean to be unpleasant, but could you maybe think a bit more before you just open your mouth and let it all fall out? Sometimes you hurt people's feelings. Girls are a lot more sensitive than us guys, you know. Boy, my big sister can break out in tears at the least little thing. Don't you have any sisters?" he asked.

"Nope! Just an older brother who left home last year. He couldn't take the arguments with my old man anymore. So, it's just me, Mom and him now." Zack was looking at the ground and scuffing his feet as he walked.

"That's sounds kinda' tough. But, it's lunch time, and I'm hungry. Com'on. Let's go get something to eat!"

"I don't think I'll be very welcome. You go ahead."

"Nope! Let's go together!" Carl put his arm lightly around Zack's shoulders, and steered him towards the Dining Hall.

Mr. Hank was standing by their table when the two boys approached. "Zack, let's talk a moment," he quietly requested. They stepped a little away from the table. "You made Lucy feel bad with your inappropriate remarks. Do you think you might be able to just say you're sorry to her?"

"Okay, if you say so." Zack shrugged and walked behind Lucy as he went to sit down. "I'm sorry!" he said out of the corner of his mouth as he passed her. Mr. Hank was watching the performance, and had to smile at the look of shock on Lucy's face as she digested what had just happened.

"Huh? Okay! Whatever!" she said.

"Hopefully, that's the end of it," he thought to himself.

Everyone settled down at the table, and by the time lunch was over, the promised rain had arrived, bringing with it thunder and lightning. Only indoor activities were on the schedule. All manner of board games were available in the Recreation Hall (The Rec.). As well, all the indoor craft buildings would be open for business as usual.

"Kids, I have some paperwork to get done. I'm going over to the admin building. That's where you can find me if you need me," Ms. C. told the group, as she stood and stepped away from the table.

"I've got some, too," Mr. Hank said. "I'll come with you. See you kids at dinner-if not before," and he followed her out the door.

The kids looked around the table at each other, a little unsettled about what to do next.

"Well, I think I'm going over to the woodworking shop," Harry announced, to no one in particular, as he stood up. "I need more practice with making wooden corners. Wanna' come Zack?"

"Nah!" was the only response from a hunched over Zack.

"I think I'm going back over to Arts and Crafts," Lucy said. "I'm really having fun with painting, and I've been thinking of a few things I'd like to add to my picture. What about you, June? Wanna' come, too?"

"I don't think so, Lucy. I'd like to challenge someone to a board game at the Rec. How about it, Shelley? You up for a game of Scrabble, or Yahtzee?"

"That sounds like fun," Shelley eagerly responded. "I'm water logged from swimming this morning, so staying in and playing a fun game sounds great. You can't go swimming in a thunderstorm anyway. What are you going to do, Carl?" she asked.

"I haven't really thought about it yet. It might be a good time to take some indoor pictures-see how I do with people," he thoughtfully responded. "You have any plans, Zack?"

"What's the big deal about everybody's plans?" was Zack's surly response.

"You just don't seem to get it, Zack." June felt compelled to figure out what was up with Zack and his unpleasant attitude. How could the poor guy enjoy anything with such a negative outlook? "We're like a small family here. We share so much of our time and space. The rest of us are having a fine time, and you are determined to be Mister Grouch at every opportunity. Com'on! What gives?"

"It ain't none of your business. I ain't hurtin' no one, and I've done all the things just like the rest of you. Can't ya just leave me alone?" Zack looked close to tears, as he pushed out the door into the deluge.

"Wow! That was something!" Carl looked thoughtfully around at the others. "You shouldn't be too hard on him, June. I don't think he has much of a home life. He said his older brother has left home, and he's the only one left. He didn't say anything about his mother, and just that his father shouts a lot. Poor kid! It doesn't sound like he has much to have a good attitude about."

"Of course, I didn't know all that. I wouldn't have said what I did if I had," June said ruefully. "But he still shouldn't just open his mouth and let fly with whatever."

"That's sad, is what it is," Lucy said. She almost felt like crying for him. "What can we do?"

"I don't know as there is much we can do," Harry said. "We can't just tell him we know about his home life. That would be betraying what he told Carl in confidence. I'm sure he wouldn't want that to be known."

"We'll have to try to overlook what he says, and maybe ask his opinion of things?" Shelley asked hesitantly.

"Sure, we can try that, but don't expect any miracles," June advised.

And with that, the kids left the Dining Hall to go to their chosen afternoon activities, each wondering a little where Zack had got to.

Zack hadn't gotten to very far. He went back to the cabin. No one was there. He sat down on his bunk. Then he rolled on to it and into a ball. His confused thoughts kept circling around in his head. Making friends, fitting in, being angry, his father's anger, being unhappy. They wore him out. He was tired from it all. Finally, he fell asleep.

About an hour later he awoke with a start. He hadn't intended to fall asleep. He wasn't a baby, needing an afternoon nap. And he didn't want anyone finding him like that. He jumped up, and was quickly out of the cabin, eager to put some distance between it and himself. He didn't pay attention to where he was going-just out of there. And it didn't matter. He ducked his head to keep the rain off his face. He had no direction in mind. He let his feet take him where they wanted to go. "What's the matter with me?" he wondered. "Why don't people like me? Why can't I make a friend? I like it here, but no one likes me." These thoughts continued to race endlessly around in his head as he walked in the rain.

Then he had a new thought-which was more a realization than a thought. He stood stalk still. "I don't want to go home, where my father is always so angry. I feel like...... I'm getting to be just like him." This was a very scary thought for Zack. "Just like dad? Oh, no, no, never!" Up 'til then he had been walking around with no attention, or even a care, to where he was, or where he was going.

Now he looked around at the dripping trees, and down at the soggy trail under his feet. '"I know where I am." The sound of his own voice-speaking aloud-was a bit of a shock, but he carried on. "This is the trail to the cave. I'm on the trail to the cave. I'll go to the cave."

Common sense told him he needed to at least get his flashlight. "I'll go back to the cabin. Everybody is doing their thing right now, and I can get in and out without seeing anyone. I'll be gone before they know I've gone." He didn't care about the rain as he put action to his thoughts and retraced his steps back to the path that led to Unit Three. Soon he had himself outfitted with flashlight, hiking boots, a jacket, his rain poncho, and some snacks he had secreted away, which were now all together in his backpack. At the last minute, he grabbed a small box of matches Mr. Hank always kept on the top of the door frame. He took a quick look out the door. Seeing no one, he slipped out into the surrounding trees, and was on his way, back to the trail he had so recently left

He actually felt a bit happy as he strode along. There was no one around that he could offend, or that he had to pay attention to. It was just he, by himself and, the uncomplaining, uncriticizing, albeit rainy, forest. He began to look around. This was the first time he had ever been in the woods alone. He walked slowly. He didn't have to keep up with anyone else. He was awed by the size of the tall trees reaching up and up into the cloudy sky. And the thick bushes crowding the spaces between the trees looked like they could hide an army in their lush undergrowth. "I like it here," he thought, and settled into a steady pace.

* * * * * * * *

Dinnertime arrived in due course, and the kids assembled at their usual table. Mr. Hank and Ms. C. came in from the admin building, dodging raindrops as best they could. "Hey, kids! Did you have fun this afternoon?" Ms. C. asked as she approached the table and took in their bright faces.

"Yeah, I got some more things into my painting, and I'm more comfortable with the oils," Lucy said.

"Me, too, I'm feeling more capable with the different ways of making wooden corners," Harry said.

"I won the first game of Scrabble," June volunteered.

"Yeah, but I won the next two," Shelley wore a big smile. "Thanks for letting me."

"I didn't let you. You won fair and square," June assured her. Shelley gave her a doubtful look, but didn't press further. It felt good to be a winner-at least for now.

Carl was fiddling around with his camera, and hadn't said anything as yet. "What about you, Carl?" Mr. Hank prompted.

"Huh? What?" There was a look of confusion on his face.

"How was your afternoon?" Mr. Hank asked. "I didn't mean to startle you."

"Oh! That's okay! I've been trying to figure out some of the settings on this camera, you know, distance and light settings-that kind of stuff. It's different than shooting in the outdoors."

"Yes, it is," Ms. C. agreed. "I'm sure you'll get the hang of it. Want to take a picture of all of us here? It would be a good souvenir for everyone."

"That's a great idea! You get more experience, and we all get a great reminder," Lucy enthused.

"Wait a minute! Where's Zack?" Harry questioned, and looked around the Dining Hall hoping to see Zack somewhere in the crowd.

"Has anyone seen him since lunch?" Mr. Hank asked, as he, too, scanned the Dining Hall.

"I don't think so," June spoke for them all. "He got upset with us and went off by himself. We didn't see him in the Rec center, did we, Shelley?"

"Nope! We'd have seen him if he came in, I'm sure."

"He didn't come with me to the woodshop, either," Harry confirmed.

"He definitely wasn't in the Arts and Crafts building," Lucy added.

"I went in most of the buildings this afternoon and I didn't happen across him," Carl said. "Maybe he just lost track of time."

"Okay! Let's give him a few more minutes," Ms. C. suggested. "We can get our own trays while we wait. The line is thinning out," she added and gestured toward the kitchen

By the time they had gotten their dinner and were all again seated at their table, there was still no sign of Zack.

"I had better tell Matt," Mr. Hank told Ms. C., as he got up from the table and made his way across the room.

"Kids, let's eat up while our dinner is still warm. We can't do anything else right now," and Ms. C. took a forkful of the lasagna. "It's as delicious as usual. Dig in!" she encouraged.

"I don't feel very hungry," Lucy quietly confided to Shelley, as the girls sat together at the far end of the table.

"Me, neither! Maybe we really hurt his feelings this afternoon," she was close to tears.

"I think we should tell Ms. C. about it," Lucy said, and she stood up from the table.

"Okay! You tell her and I'll back you up. Com'on, June," and she explained what they were going to do.

"I'm in," she said and stood to join them.

"Ms. C.?" Lucy began, as they approached the other end of the table where Ms. C. had been sitting with Mr. Hank. "We have something to tell you," and she did, while the others listened and nodded their heads to verify the story.

"Thank you very much, kids, for telling me. You all stay put here. I'll go and speak with Mr. Hank and Mr. Matt. Finish your dinner. I'll be back! And don't worry," she assured them.

"How can we not worry? We might be responsible for causing Zack to do something foolish." Carl was visibly upset.

Harry put his hand on Carl's shoulder. "Take it easy, Carl! Zack's not a stupid kid, and he seems like he can take care of himself. I don't think he's going to do anything really crazy. Let's finish dinner while we wait to hear back from Mr. Hank, okay?"

"Yeah! I guess so. We can't do much else right now," Carl answered as they all watched the counsellors and Mr. Matt leave the Dining Hall.

The table was very quiet as the kids sat back down and tried to eat, each with their own thoughts and worries. Only about twenty minutes had passed before Mr. Hank and Ms. C. were back with them, though it seemed like hours. "Okay, kids, here's what we are going to do," Mr. Hank began. "We are going to do a complete search of all the camp areas, buildings, cabins, bath houses, sports areas, the waterfront. Mr. Matt has notified the local police. They are coming here to help in the search, and with search dogs, especially in the woods. They will want to talk with your kids as well. They will also check all over town and question shop personnel. They will have a plan for their search. So, you kids need to go to your cabins and stay put, okay?"

"But we can help. We know what he looks like," June protested for them all.

"The searchers will have pictures, and you don't want to add to the confusion by getting in the way. They will be looking for ONE missing boy, and don't need to be bumping into other kids in their search," Ms. C. reasoned.

"Yeah, that makes sense," Harry said. "Okay! Let's go gang. We'll go to our cabins, Mr. Hank," he acquiesced.

"Yes, Harry. And please stay there," he responded. While the crestfallen kids headed back to their Unit, he and Ms. C. returned to the office to join the group of searchers. They would be helpful, along with the other counsellors, as leaders of the various groups that would soon be assembling and assigned specific areas to search. It was going to be a long night.

CHAPTER TEN

It was nearly midnight when the search was called off. Wet and weary searchers gathered in the Dining Hall where hot drinks and sandwiches awaited them. Disappointment and discouragement were heavy in the air. The most positive thing they could say was that none of them had come across a damaged or dead body. They had done their best under the circumstances and conditions. There was also refreshment for the bedraggled hounds who had done their best as well. They would all get some rest, and wait for daylight to continue, and expand, their search. The rangers from the Wildlife Refuge would be called in. They had more intimate knowledge of the mountainous terrain that surrounded them.

* * * * * * * *

Zack had had a good head start on the searchers in the time it had taken them to get organized. He had no trouble, in spite of the rain, following the same path they had taken not two days ago up the mountain of the caves-Mount Gregory he remembered. He liked the name. It sounded strong. Somewhere along the way he had picked up a stout stick-a fallen tree limb-that he broke down to just the right height to be a good walking stick. It was very helpful as he made his way up the rain slick, and muddy, trail.

The longer he walked, the better he felt. It was the first time in his life that he had truly been alone. It didn't scare him at all, not even when he realized the light was getting dimmer. He felt only a deep sense of relief. Even his body felt physically better-never mind that he was toiling up the side of a mountain in the rain. He began to think about that. He pondered the sensation. "Why am I feeling better?" he thought. "What's making a difference?" Then he remembered what he had been thinking about earlier in the day-his father's angry ways-his shouting, and his realization that he was beginning to mimic them. That had truly frightened him. If he became like his father, he wouldn't want to live.

He stopped and stood as still as a statue. There happened to be a large rock just there, next to the trail. Zack plopped down on it. "My father! He isn't here, and I won't have to see him for quite a while. I won't have to hear him ranting and raving about anything and nothing. I don't have to be afraid of what he is going to be like when he comes home from work-what he's going to find fault with. I'm feeling free! That's what I'm feeling!" It was with a new found lightness that Zack jumped up from the rock and, with a smile a mile wide-that no one would ever see, he continued on.

* * * * * * * * *

The kids in Unit Three had not had a good night. When Mr. Hank and Ms. C. had returned so late with no Zack and no happy news, it was nearly impossible to go to sleep. Worry and 'what ifs' kept them awake. Mr. Hank and Ms. C. were adamant, however, that they go to bed and at least rest and stay quiet.

"Also," Ms. C. explained to them just before the girls headed to their own cabin, and lights out, "tomorrow you kids are going to be with the Unit One kids. Their counselors are Mr. Jack and Ms. Hockman. You have met them, around camp..."

"Yeah!" Harry interrupted. Mr. Jack runs the wood shop and..."

"To continue," Ms. C. said, and interrupted him right back, giving him a stern look as well, "and will get together with them after breakfast. I'm sure you will have as fine a day with them as you do with us."

When the sun appeared early the next morning, the rain clouds were gone, and the world was a-sparkle with fresh washed greenery, as last night's groups reassembled, before the campers were up. They were introduced to Rangers Harry Brown and Ginger Curtis who had joined them for the continued search.

Matt had an announcement: "I spoke with Zack's parents last night. His mother was quite worried. I assured her that we were doing everything possible, and that there were no hungry bears or wild animals that might harm him. His father was angry. He said his son could take care of himself-'What's all the fuss about?' I tried to assure him, but he said he had to go to work, and he hung up. Well, we know what we have to do. Let's get going."

The rangers had area maps for everyone. The maps showed the many trails that criss–crossed the surrounding mountains. So, after a quick breakfast and hot drinks, the searchers continued in groups as before. They also carried lunches that had been packed by the Dining Hall kitchen staff.

"Shelley, Lucy?" June's quiet voice got their attention-none of them was asleep. "I have an idea. Let's get Harry and Carl."

"Okay! I'll go get them," Lucy offered. She quickly stuffed her feet into her slippers and dashed out of the cabin. She was back minutes later with the boys in tow

"What's up?" Carl asked

"Lucy said you have an idea, June?" Harry queried.

"Yeah! It may be a crazy one, but I think Zack may have gone up to the caves," June looked around at their faces.

"What makes you think that?" Harry asked.

"Don't you remember how mesmerized he was when we saw those stalactites and such? He had no harsh words to say the whole time we were in the caves," June said.

"Yes, that's right. He explored on his own, and not a grouch or a grump at all. I guess we didn't really think about it at the time because we were all so entranced as well." Lucy explained.

"I think you're on to something, June," Carl agreed. "What's your idea?"

"We should go up and look for him," Shelley exclaimed for her. "That's a great idea."

"Wait a minute," Harry broke in. "How are we going to do that? We have to report to Unit One."

"I have that all figured out," June assured them. "We go to breakfast as usual-be sure to stuff some extra food into your pockets-and then we tell Ms. Hockman and Mr. Jack that we'd like to go to our individual activities. They surely can't object to that. So, then we meet back here, gather some stuff-our flashlights, jackets, some rope-can you find some Carl? You've been wandering around everywhere here at the Retreat."

"What do we need rope for?" Shelley asked.

"Well, we are here in the mountains and you never know when a rope might come in handy," Harry filled in for June.

"Oh, yeah, you're right. I wasn't focused," she admitted.

"Any questions?" June asked.

"How about some extra food for Zack-if we find him? He'll be sure to be hungry," Lucy said.

"Good thinking, Lucy. I'll pilfer some while I'm scouting for rope. I'm pretty sure I can cadge some from someone in the kitchen," Carl promised.

"Okay, gang, breakfast. Then let's get to work. Meet back here by nine o'clock with your stuff, and don't forget your flashlights," June instructed, sounding like a drill master. No one took offense. They were hyped and ready to look for, and hopefully, find Zack, safe and sound.

* * * * * * * *

And Zack **was** safe and sound at that very moment. He didn't have a watch, but he figured it was at least five, maybe six, hours, before he had made it to the cave. As the trail got steeper, it had gotten slipperier as well. For every few feet he went up, he would eventually slide back down, but he persevered. The rain had finally tapered off, and the sky had cleared to reveal a nearly full moon. Zack had stopped and sat on a handy rock to gaze up at the sky. 'Wow! What a sight!' he thought. It wasn't easy to see much of the night sky in the city because of all the earthbound bright lights. Here, the sky was magnificent. 'Maybe I'll become an astronomer,' he thought. He sat on his rock for a long time, resting, and staring at the glorious sky, enjoying the quiet of the mountains.

Finally, the chill of his damp clothes and the cool of the night air caused him to shiver and rouse from his rock. He trudged on upward, and was nearly at the end of his endurance when the huge rock pile that held the entrance to the cave finally came into view. Zack sagged in relief. He took a few minutes to regain his breath, before squeezing around the final boulder blocking the way. He fished his flashlight out of his pack and pushed past the greenery hanging down from above. The darkness of the cave was broken by the flashlight's narrow beam, and illuminated a rough bench-like rock shelf at the base of the smooth side wall. Zack sank down on the shelf, took off his pack, and laid down, putting his head on his pack. In minutes, he was snoring.

* * * * * * * *

At nine o'clock, June was standing outside the girls' cabin, pacing up and down, anxious that Harry and Carl would soon appear with their gear and provisions. Shelley and Lucy were in the cabin, putting their packs together. They were nearly ready. June wanted them to be gone before any counsellor came looking for them.

"Hey, June, here we are," Carl called out as he and Harry appeared on the path from their cabin. "I got some rope from the waterfront." He lifted it from his shoulder to demonstrate. "Peter said they had some they didn't need. He asked what I wanted it for, and I told him we were marking out the sport field for some competition games. I think he sort'ta believed me. I told him I would return it when we were done."

"Good thinking, Carl, and you got some extra food from the kitchen?" she inquired.

"He sure did!" Harry said. "And then some. We have enough for a small army."

"Well, not quite that much, but we don't know what's going to happen, and we should be prepared," Carl defended the slight overload. "I just asked for box lunches, said we wanted to have a picnic. It worked like a charm."

Just then, Shelley and Lucy emerged from the cabin, all outfitted for the day's trek. "Ta-da," and Lucy struck a pose like a headliner.

"Lovely!" was June's only comment. "Okay, gang, I have left a note for Ms. C. to let her know where we have gone. She won't find it too soon, and maybe we will even be back with Zack by then."

"You look like the best dressed mountain climber I have ever seen," Carl commented, and it won a smile from Lucy.

"Okay, okay, let's stop fooling around. Pass out those lunches, Carl. We can each carry our own, and let's get going. Time's a wastin," June reminded them.

"Yes, ma'am!" And Harry gave a salute, stuck his lunch in his pack, slung it his on his back, and strode off down the trail.

Lucy fell in line, then Shelley, Carl, and last was June, who brought up the rear.

* * * * * * * *

When Zack awoke, he felt a moment of fear. This was definitely not his bunk in the cabin, or his bed at home. Then it began to come back, the argument at camp, the rain, and the trek up the mountain in the wet, the cave. He was in the cave. It was pitch black. He had no idea what time it was. He fumbled around in his pack for his flashlight. That was better. He shone it around and saw the entrance and the hanging greenery. It was dark outside as well. He stood and walked over to push aside some of the greenery and get a look at the sky. Yep, the stars were still up there, but they were beginning to fade. 'It must be getting on to morning,' he thought. He went back to his pack and fished around inside for the snacks he had brought. It wasn't much of a breakfast, but it was all he had. Then he needed a bathroom break outside. It had gotten a bit lighter already.

Back inside Zack walked further into the cavern to where the ceiling opened up overhead. The vastness overwhelmed him as it had before. He shone his flashlight at the towering mites and tites. He was just as spellbound this second time seeing them as he had been the first. He stood stock still to admire each one.

Then, at the edge of light from his flashlight he noticed a very dark area. From their hike here he remembered there were some small side caves. He moved his light towards it and headed over to get a better look. It **was** a small side cave, and the entrance was not quite as tall as Zack. He had to bend down to look inside. He could see that it went into the mountainside quite a way. 'I wouldn't like to meet any mountain critter in there,' he thought.

He continued to explore the main cave, his flashlight picking out the different colors of all the stalactites and stalagmites-each a wonder of its own. He lost track of time as he wandered throughout the cave complex. His flashlight also picked out a couple more small side caves, but, as with the first one, Zack didn't enter any of them. He had no desire to unexpectedly meet any mountain creatures, though he had heard no sounds to indicate that such critters were actually there.

But, suddenly Zack did hear a sound, one he had not expected to hear. It was voices, and they didn't sound friendly. In fact, they sounded just the opposite, angry, and arguing. He was all too familiar with those sounds. The angry voices were coming closer. He could see shadows cast by lights the voices must be carrying. 'Time to explore one of those side caves,' Zack thought, and he backed into the nearest one. The voices were coming closer. Now he could make out the words.

"Buck said the skins were in a small side cave inside a much bigger cave," one man said.

"I know what he said, Guy," a second voice said in a whiny voice. "But what makes you think it's this cave?"

"Look, stupid, we are running out of caves to search. Just shut up and keep looking." The second voice was ugly. It sounded just like Zack's father at his ugliest.

Zack backed further into his hideaway. "I hope no snakes are in here," he thought. Just then he stumbled over some fallen rocks, which tumbled with a sharp smack. Zack held his breath.

"What was that?" the first voice called out, fear evident in the words.

"What, you scared of your own shadow, Willy?" Guy sneered. "This is a cave. Anything could be in here, snakes, bats, maybe even a bear."

"I didn't sign on to get eaten by no bear," Willy's voice had a quaver in it.

"Oh, shut up and just keep looking. The sooner we check this out, the sooner we may be rich. You ain't forgotten that, have ya'?" he challenged.

"No, I ain't forgotten, but I'd like to be alive to enjoy my riches."

"Yeah, yeah, just get on with it."

Zack slowly let out the breath he had been holding. "Whew, that was close!" When the sounds of the searchers receded, he cautiously crept from his hiding place, feeling his way along the side wall. At the entrance to his small cave he briefly directed his light-his fingers hiding most of it-away from the searchers. Sounds are magnified in a cave, so he would be able to tell if they came his way again. He definitely didn't want to reveal himself. He didn't like what he had heard. It didn't sound like these were good guys. Maybe they wouldn't stay very long. The only problem, for now, was that they were between him and the main entrance.

* * * * * * * * *

Meanwhile, the Unit Three kids were trudging up Mount Gregory. The rain had left the ground on the lower trail soft and squishy, but that didn't hinder the kids. They were on a mission. In no time they were headed upwards. There were a few slippery places to carefully navigate, but nothing a group of healthy, strong, and determined young people couldn't handle. That's not to say there was no huffing and puffing to be heard.

After what seemed like a fairly long amount of time, Harry stopped in a clearing and looked at his watch. "Hey, June," he called down to her. She was still bringing up the rear. "It's quarter after ten. Let's stop for a short break, take a drink of water and maybe have a snack," he suggested.

"Good idea, Harry!" she called back. "I'll be right up."

One by one, Lucy, Shelley, and Carl reached Harry's rest stop and spread out around the clearing, glad for the pause in the climb. June wasn't very far behind. "Whew!" she exclaimed, as she plunked down on a fat rock beside the trail. "I think we are doing great, and I'm glad it isn't too hot today. The rain seems to have cooled things down a bit."

"The mountains always seem cool to me," Shelley said, "and they smell so good-clean and a little spicy. It must be all these pine trees," and she waved her arm at all the giants around them.

"I'll second that," Carl agreed. "I'd like to take some of this air home for my mom," he added. "If only!"

"That would be great," Lucy said wistfully. "If you figure out a way to do it, let me know, okay?"

"Sure thing, Luce," he assured her with a grin.

"Okay, break time is over," June announced after about ten minutes. "I think we are about half way there, so……"

"Yeah, I think so, too," Harry broke in.

June gave him a withering stare… "We shouldn't need another rest until we make the top," she finished. "Let's get going!"

"Yes, sir, boss," Harry nodded, a bit chagrined, and shouldered his pack. "Onward and upward."

With a few groans, all the rest fell in line.

In spite of a few sore leg muscles, and achy shoulders, everyone was glad to be on the move again. The prospect of finding Zack spurred them on.

* * * * * * * *

Zack, hindered by the fear of being discovered if he used his flashlight full on, was slowly creeping further from the main entrance. He had suddenly remembered seeing the hole in the top, the ceiling of the cave, when they had been here before. It was awesome. Maybe he could climb out from there. But it wasn't easy to find his way with the meager light he allowed himself to use. Well, there wasn't much choice unless he wanted to spend another night in the cave. And by then his flashlight would probably be dead-even if he wasn't.

Zack would have been somewhat comforted if he had known that Guy and Willy had left the cave to get some fresh air. The cave reminded them too much of time spent behind bars. Willy was especially claustrophobic-he trembled at the thought of small, confined spaces. He had started to perspire profusely, soaking his shirt in no time at all, perspiration running down his face, obscuring his vision. He began stumbling over all the rocks on the floor of the cave. Panic wasn't far behind.

"What's the matter with you?" Guy grunted at him. "You're making enough noise to bring in the fuzz."

"I can't help it, Guy! Places like this give me the heebie-jeebies. I gotta get outta here." Willy was practically crying.

"Okay, okay! Hold your pants on. We go out and sit for a time. Then we come back in. Does that suit you tender sensitivities?" Guy sneered.

"Yeah, yeah, let's do that," Willy hastily agreed, and made a beeline for where he was sure the cave entrance was.

"Hey, stupid! You're going the wrong way." Guy grabbed the back of Willy's soaked shirt. "This way!"

"Okay, okay! Just get me outta here!" Willy's teeth had even begun to chatter.

They stumbled and fumbled their way to the cave entrance. Willy gave a sigh of relief and sank down on the stony ground. "Thanks, Guy. You're a real pal."

"Yeah, yeah," he wasn't interested in being a 'real pal'. He was wondering how he got saddled with such a whiner. "Look, if you don't want to get rich, Willy, sit out here in the nice warm sunshine, or run down the mountain calling for your mama," using the ugly voice that had reminded Zack so much of his father.

"Why ya' treating me so mean, Guy? I can't help how I'm feeling," Willy pleaded. "I'm doing my best," he whined.

"Aw, shut up, ya wimpy baby. We got a job to do, and if you want any of the rewards of that job, you'll help. Otherwise, get outta my face and don't bother me no more." Guy turned his back on Willy, walked to the edge of the mountain top, and gazed out over the valley. He couldn't care less about the beauty around him. His whole purpose of being in this situation was finding the furs Buck had promised were there.

* * * * * * * *

By this time, the kids were nearing the top of the mountain. "Whew! I was beginning to think we were never going to get here," Shelley said.

"Well, we aren't there yet," June pointed out, "but really close," she encouraged. "There's still that rock mound to get around."

"Shhh!" Carl, who was in the lead, held out his arm and warned them with a finger over his mouth. "Listen!" he whispered.

Silence fell and they did just that. "What did you hear?" whispered Harry, when he heard nothing at all.

"I thought I heard some guys speaking kinda cross," Carl whispered back. "Stay right here and I'll go take a look." Carl quietly took off his pack and crept forward. As he approached the last large rock blocking the way, he heard the last of Guy's words, and got a glimpse of the top of his head as he walked to the mountain's edge. Carl quickly crouched down. He didn't think the big man had seen him. He quietly edged his way back to the others. "I think there are at least two guys there, though I only saw the top of one head. I don't think he was talking to himself. His voice was nasty sounding."

"Do you think he knows we are here?" Lucy sounded worried.

"I don't think so. He was just standing looking out over the mountains," Carl said.

"Okay, so what should we do?" Shelley asked no one in particular.

"I don't think we should confront them," June advised.

"I agree," Harry said, "especially if they are not happy sounding. What are they doing up here anyway?" he wondered. "And they would wonder the same about us," he added, ruefully.

"We can't just walk up to them and announce that we are looking for our friend," June was thinking hard.

"Hey," Lucy was excited. "Remember that hole we found in the top of the cave, where all the light was coming in? That has to be up on top of that whole, humongous rock pile. We can climb up there and look for it. We have the rope and we can climb down and check it out. What do you think?" She looked around at all their faces.

"Lucy, that's a super idea," June enthused.

"Yeah, it was a good size hole, from the bottom looking up. We should be able to find it," Carl was excited.

"We sure have to try," Harry agreed. "But we need to be very careful as we look-that we don't get too excited and fall in it. It could be well camouflaged from up there," he warned. "And we don't want to alert those angry guys, either," he reminded them.

* * * * * * * *

While all that was happening outside, Zack had been taking each step, as cautiously as he could, inside. Then he suddenly realized he was no longer hearing any stumbling noises, and no angry voices. 'Have they gone?' he wondered. He stood very still for a minute or two. All was silent. He breathed out in relief. Yep, they must have gone away. His next steps were not so carefully placed, and he moved forward more quickly. It felt good. However, just as he was truly hoping he had heard the last of them, the voices returned, and though they were not very clear, they seemed to be coming his way-coming towards where Zack stood, seemingly frozen in place, seemingly hypnotized. Then he came to and gave himself a good shake. 'I can't stand here like a scarecrow,' he thought. 'That ceiling hole can't be far now.' He forged on. And he was right. The ceiling hole hadn't been very far. Within his next few steps, Zack could see that the cave was getting lighter. His heart gave a happy jump. He turned off his light as he moved forward.

Back out front, Guy and Willy were ending their rest break. "Are ya' happy now?" Guy snarled at Willy. "Had enough of this fresh mountain air? Ready to man up and get to work?"

"You don't have to rub it in, Guy," Willy said. "I'm doing my share. Let's get it over with. There can't be that much more of that cave to check," and he picked up his pack and headed back into the darkness.

"I don't want to hear no more whining," Guy warned.

"Yeah! Yeah!" was Willy's final comment as they switched on their flashlights once more to continue their search.

* * * * * * * *

Meanwhile, back at the Retreat, the search teams had regathered to give reports on areas they had searched that morning, and the failed results of each one. They were discouraged, and getting more worried by the hour. Hank and Beth excused themselves from the group to go check in with the Unit One counsellors and the rest of their kids.

Althea and Jack from Unit One also had no good news for Hank and Beth. "We haven't seen any of your kids all morning," a worried Althea told them, "and not a word either."

"That's right," Jack affirmed with a very concerned look on his face. "I went out to your cabins just after nine o'clock, and there was no sign of them. I asked around the camp. The kitchen staff said they had given them box lunches. Carl told them they were going to have a picnic. And I went to the waterfront. Carl had also asked Peter if he could borrow a rope from him-something about using it to mark off areas on the sports field."

"I'm going back to check in the cabin," Beth said. "It's very possible there is a note somewhere there. June is a very responsible girl. I think she would do something like that-at least I'm hoping," and she hurried off.

In just a few minutes she was back, waving a piece of paper as she rushed up. "Yes, here it is," she was excited. "June did leave a note. She said they are going up to the caves we explored the other day. The kids remembered how awed Zack had been by the experience, and they felt that is a place he might think of in his unhappy state."

"Thank goodness! Now we have a good lead," Matt said. "They just might be right. Where are Rangers Brown and Curtis," he called out.

"Here we are," and Ranger Brown raised his hand above the crowd as he made his way forward, followed closely by Ranger Curtis. "We haven't had a chance to go check out those caves ourselves, yet."

"That's right!" Ranger Curtis verified. "Now seems like the perfect time to do so, and we can try out the new, motorized mountain bikes the service got just last week."

"I had forgotten about those-they'd be the perfect transport-and quicker than by foot," Ranger Brown confirmed. "We may not be able to use them all the way up, depending on the slope. But we are going to find that out. It will be a good test for them. Let's get to it, Ginger," and with a nod to his partner they put action to their words.

"Well, we don't have such vehicles, so we'll head on up from here. You can catch us up before we get to the top, I'm sure," Beth called after them.

They waved acknowledgment and were gone.

"Those kids are our responsibility," Hank spoke seriously. "We need to go up there and get them back safely. Perhaps Officers Kettering and Blackwell will come with us."

"That's a great idea," Beth agreed

"I'll round them up while you get packs ready, Beth, Okay?"

"Sounds like a good plan. Let's meet at the campfire pit at your cabin in half an hour. Will that be enough time to get everything ready-First Aid Kit, food, emergency supplies?" she questioned.

"I think so. Nurse Kathy has all that stuff ready all the time, and the kitchen staff are great in emergencies," Hank assured her with a smile. "Let's hustle." And he was off to find the Officers in question.

Beth hastened to the cabins to put together personal packs of blankets, dry socks, sweet snacks, bug spray, and anything else she could think of that might be helpful for kids who have been climbing a mountain all day. When she arrived at the campfire pit, at the appointed time, she was pleased to see Hank and the Officers ready and anxious to get underway.

* * * * * * * * *

On the mountain top, Harry was leading the climb up the back side of that gigantic rock pile, very slowly picking his way and advising the others to stay in his footsteps as much as possible. It was slow going, but they were making good progress, and were helping each other over any really difficult stretches. Ever upward they worked their way.

Little did they know that just then, below them, Zack had just made his way through the last darkness of the cave to stand under the hole in the ceiling, and gaze up into the brilliant blue sky.

They also didn't know that the two unpleasant guys were also slowly approaching the same location, though they were going more slowly as they stopped to examine each small side cave-and each time were disappointed when no cache of illegal furs awaited them. Guy's attitude did not improve with each disappointment. He took his frustration out on Willy, calling him every negative word he could think of. As the voices got louder and nearer Zack became desperate to find a good place to hide himself before they finally arrived under the hole in the roof.

"Psst!" Zack was startled. "Psst! Up here!" came a whisper. "Zack, up here!" came again. Zack looked up, way up to the rim of the ceiling gap. He nearly tumbled over when he saw Harry's face silhouetted against the sky. Then Lucy's appeared, then Carl's and Shelley's and June's.

Just at that moment, Guy stepped into the circle of light. If he was surprised to see a young man standing there, he covered it up in is usual ugly way, "What you doing in here, Kid. You been stealing things don't belong to you? You seen some bales of furs in here? Com'on kid speak up! Cat got your tongue?"

"Ah, leave the kid alone, Guy! He look like he's got a cache of furs on him?" Willy interrupted. "He looks too scared to say anything. You're scaring him. Look, kid, you know anything about any furs you best tell us."

Zack looked from one to the other of these ugly guys. The second guy wasn't as tough as the first guy-the one that was so like his father. Just looking at his ugly face caused Zack's anger to rage through him. His face darkened. His eyes blazed. He couldn't seem to get away from his no-good father. His hands balled involuntarily into fists.

Seeing the change come over Zack, Guy pulled out a long rusted hunting knife and brandished it in his face. "So, ya got nothing to say, Laddie? This knife can get pretty persuasive," and Guy advanced a step towards Zack. Zack took a step backwards. Guy advanced again. With each backward step Zack took he moved further away from the edge of the sky hole, and Guy advanced closer to that sensitive spot. His focus was securely on Zack and no thought came to him to look up. Willy had yet to reach a spot where he could see the sky, or be seen by the kids above.

From their unique position, the kids had been silently witnessing the events below. Now Harry motioned for them to back off from the rim. He took the rope from Carl and together they tied it around the trunk of a good-sized tree growing not far off. Harry dragged the rest of it close to the sky hole. Then, with hand signals he pantomimed dropping large rocks down on the big guy that was threatening Zack with the ugly knife. All nodded in agreement, and each kid scanned the ground looking for the most lethal rocks they could find and manage. In seconds, they had collected a small pile of good-sized weapons: rocks a large as footballs to rain down upon the enemy. One by one the missiles fell through the hole. And one by one they landed hard on, and all around Guy. He collapsed under the onslaught, and lay as still as those missiles. Willy stood, mouth agape, at what he has just seen.

Harry dropped the rope through the hole and quickly slid down, followed by Carl. Zack had fallen upon Guy's inert body as soon as it hit the ground, and wrested the knife from his hand. He immediately turned on Willy. "Don't get any funny ideas, mister. I got a pretty good arm for throwing things. And I ain't shy. Just sit down right here next to sleeping beauty," and he gestured with the ugly knife to the fallen rocks. "We'll get to you shortly." Then he quickly turned to Harry and Carl. "What do we do now," he asked.

The girls had slid down the rope by this time, and were also standing around the boys, avoiding getting too near either man, and wondering the same thing.

"There's plenty of extra rope here," Harry said. "Cut off a couple lengths a few feet long, and we can tie these guys up," Harry said. "And then we wait.

"What are we waiting for?" Zack asked with a puzzled look on his face, as he began sawing at the rope with the knife

"Well," June spoke up, "I left a note for Ms. C. and told her we were coming up here looking for you. I'm sure she has found the note by now, and help is on the way."

"We won't have to wait too long," Lucy added, "but I think one of us should be down at the entrance to greet whoever comes and show them the way."

"I'll do that," Shelley offered. "I really love the mountain air. This cave can be pretty stuffy." She gave a little wave as she took out her flashlight and headed into the blackness of the cave.

"Go for it, Shelley," Carl encouraged her, as he took the first length of rope Zack offered, wound it around Guy's hands, and pulled it tight. "I knew all those Boy Scout knots would come in handy sometime," he muttered under his breath. "Turn around," he ordered Willy, "and put your hands behind your back." He took the second length of rope from Zack.

Willy, who was too confused by all that was happening to do anything but what he was told, allowed himself to be tied up as well.

Shelley reached the main cave entrance and stepped outside, happy to be in the sunshine. She sat down on a handy rock and raised her face to the sun. The mountain top was a very quiet place, and bird song came clearly to her ears. But, wait, that sound is too steady to be birds-and it's really a buzzing sound. She got up from her perch and squeezed past that hindering boulder that blocked the trail from the cave's entrance. She ventured a little further down the trail. Now it was clear that the buzzing sound was from some sort of machine, or vehicle, maybe an electric saw? She stood still, listening, as the sound got nearer and nearer. Then she could see a patch of red through the trees. Then a helmeted person on an unusual looking motor bike, and then another one. Shelley jumped up and down in excitement. "Hello! Hello," she called out, and waved her arms.

The first person stopped a few feet in front of her, with the second one right behind. The first person removed his helmet. "Well, hello yourself. I think you must be one of the kids we are looking for," he said. "I'm Ranger Brown, and this," he began as the second person got off her bike, "is Ranger Curtis. We were told you might be up here. I understand there is supposed to be a cave around here somewhere, but I don't see one." Both Rangers wore puzzled expressions.

"You understand perfectly, Ranger Brown. I'm Shelley, and I'm here to greet you and show you the way. Follow me." Shelley was all business now. Time for explanations later. "Wait!" she turned back. "Do you have flashlights with you?"

"Oh, yes, we do!" Ranger Curtis said, and both Rangers took lights from their packs. "Let's go!"

Shelley was quite comfortable with the cave by now and easily led the little group to the hole in the ceiling clearing. Expecting to find only kids, the Rangers were quite surprised to see too unsavory looking characters tied up and laying on the cave floor amidst a jumble of rocks.

"What have we here?" Ranger Brown questioned with a frown on his face.

"Um, well," Harry began, "when we got up there," and he pointed up to the skylight, "I saw this guy here," and he toed Guy with his foot. "He was threatening our friend," and he pointed at Zack, "with a wicked ugly knife. We came up here looking for Zack, and didn't expect to find anything, or anyone, but him."

"Yeah, that's right." June broke in. "We knew Zack wasn't happy and he had liked the cave when we first saw it. We thought he might have come up here to do some thinking, and...."

"When we got here and heard these two dudes out front arguing, we remembered this hole in the ceiling, and decided to come in this way," Carl continued.

"And that's when we saw these guys picking on Zack," Lucy added. "The only thing we could think of to do was drop some rocks on them-so we did."

Now the kids fell silent. The Rangers were a bit speechless as well, and stood shaking their heads.

"We aren't in any bad trouble are we?" Shelley asked with a tremble in her voice.

"I'm sure you aren't, but we will have to get this all sorted out when we get down off this mountain," Ranger Curtis assured them.

Just then, a loud "HELLO!' was heard from the front of the cave.

"That sounded like Ms. C.", June said. "I'll go and bring her, and whoever, back here," she added. "Um, may I?"

"Yes, please," Ranger Brown affirmed. "We have been expecting them-and some officers."

In no time, June was back with Ms. C., Mr. Hank and two officers.

"Whoa! What's all this?" Mr. Hank stopped short and stood with his hands on his hips.

"Hey, those two guys look like the dudes that have been hanging out in town asking about caves," Officer Kettering said in surprise.

"Well, they were doing more than just 'asking,'" Ranger Curtis said, and she went on to relate what the kids had told them.

"Well, that's a whole different kettle of fish." Officer Blackwell said. "We need to get these guys down the mountain, tended to for injuries, and then into jail until we find out what's what."

With a minimum of time and trouble, additional security arrived to take control and possession of Guy and Willy. As soon as he came to, Guy began swearing and arguing that he was innocent, he was just exploring a dumb old cave, and he wanted a lawyer. Willy just kept his mouth shut.

For the rest of their two weeks, the kids did what summer camp kids do. But now they felt they were more of a team. "One for all and all for one!" Zack could hardly believe that all the others had come to his rescue. He doubted that he would ever forget what they did-especially after he had been so unpleasant to them so often. And it was a lesson he would never forget as well-even though he couldn't think of the words to say. He would let his actions show how he felt from now on. Maybe some of it would rub off on his old man.

And he was definitely going to spread the word about Tuckaway Retreat- where you could have great fun and adventures, find out new things about yourself, and best of all, make new friends that you will never forget, even if you never see them again. But, who knows, maybe you will.

THE END